A Note to Readers

While the Borlands and their friends are fictional, the Easter riots actually took place. After the Civil War, there was increasing tension between people who owned companies and the people who worked for them. Some owners did not care if their employees were working in dangerous places. They refused to pay their workers enough money to live on.

Because of these problems, workers formed unions. They thought if they worked together against company owners, they would have a better chance of getting more pay and safer working conditions. Sometimes they were successful. Many times they were not. And too often, violence erupted.

In most places, unions weren't legal. Sometimes company owners paid people to break up the unions. Many union members were killed, and some union members killed company supporters in return. This conflict went on for decades. It wasn't until 1935 that the federal government passed a law guaranteeing workers the right to form unions.

Rachel
and the Riot

THE LABOR MOVEMENT
DIVIDES A FAMILY

SUSAN MARTINS MILLER

BARBOUR
PUBLISHING

ISBN 1-59310-355-7

Cover design by Lookout Design Group, Inc.

Published by Barbour Publishing, Inc., P.O. Box 719, Uhrichsville, Ohio 44683, www.barbourbooks.com

Our mission is to publish and distribute inspirational products offering exceptional value and biblical encouragement to the masses.

 Member of the
Evangelical Christian
Publishers Association

Printed in the United States of America.
5 4 3 2 1

CONTENTS

CHAPTER 1

Papa's News

"Pass me that knife, please."

Ten-year-old Rachel Borland wiped her hands on the white apron that covered her blue-and-white-checked dress and pushed her blond hair away from her blue eyes. Then she arranged six carrots on the thick butcher block next to the sink. Potatoes, onions, and shelled peas were already lined up along the counter.

Sam, her twelve-year-old brother, handed her the knife. "What are you making?"

"Stew." Chunks of beef simmered in a big black pot on the stove. Rachel was ready to add the vegetables. She checked the flame on the new gas stove.

"Do you have to put in onions?" Sam asked, making a sour face.

"Papa likes onions. You can pick them out."

"You sound just like Mama."

Sam lifted the lid on the pot and bent his dark head over it to inspect the meat. Sam took after their French grandmother. His hair and eyes were as dark as Rachel's were fair.

"Why don't you stir that, as long as you have the lid off?" Rachel handed her brother a spoon.

"Do you think Papa will be home on time?" Sam asked. "I don't like burned stew."

"He hasn't telephoned," Rachel answered. "He tries to call if he knows he has to stay late at the hospital."

Sam slumped into a chair at the kitchen table. "When your father is a doctor, you have to get used to unpredictable hours."

"That's what Mama always says." Rachel attacked the carrots and whacked them into bite-sized pieces. "But Uncle Ernest is a banker, and he works long hours, too," she added, using the title her parents insisted the children use as a sign of respect toward their older cousins.

"Downtown Minneapolis is a busy place to do business."

"Uncle Ernest says it's busier every year. He can hardly believe it's 1889 already."

"And Uncle Stanley works for the railroad," Sam added. "And his shifts change all the time." He glanced at the pot. "Just don't burn the stew."

Rachel rolled her eyes.

Mama came through the door from the dining room.

"How are you doing with supper?"

Rachel scooped up a handful of carrots and threw them in the pot. "Everything is on schedule. We just need Papa to come home." She added the potatoes to the pot and stirred the mixture vigorously.

"Put the peas in last," Mama said. "They don't take long to cook."

"I remember." Rachel added the onions and left the peas on the counter.

"I'm sure Papa will be here soon." Mama opened a cupboard and removed a stack of large bowls. "Sam, can you get the spoons, please?"

Sam stood up and crossed the kitchen. Just as he pulled open a drawer, they heard the front door open.

"There's Papa," Rachel said. She wiped her hands on her apron again and went to greet her father.

"Right on time," Mama said.

Mama and Sam followed Rachel to the front door. Eight-year-old Carrie was already there with her arms around her father's neck. He scooped up his youngest child and turned to greet his family.

"Something smells wonderful," Papa said.

"Rachel's making stew," Mama informed him.

Papa looked at Rachel. "You're becoming quite a cook, young lady."

"I made baking powder biscuits, too," Rachel said proudly.

"I can see that." Papa reached out and wiped a smudge of flour from Rachel's cheek.

"Will you sit next to me at supper, Papa?" Carrie asked.

Papa smiled. "Don't I always?"

"I was just making sure."

"We weren't certain that you would be home on time tonight," Mama said.

Papa put Carrie down and sighed. "I wasn't either. The streetcar drivers are threatening to strike."

"A strike?"

"Why?"

"What's a strike?"

"How would we get downtown?"

"One question at a time," Papa said, holding up one hand. "I'll tell you everything I know."

Rachel glanced back toward the kitchen and sat on the edge of a chair.

"You already know," Papa said, "that the streetcar drivers have formed a union. They think that if they bind themselves together as one voice, then they will have more power. They want a raise in their wages."

"They haven't had a raise in a long time," Mama said. "Your cousin Stanley reminds us of that all the time."

"But Thomas Lowry, the owner of the Minneapolis Street Railway, says the company is losing money," Papa said. "He can't even afford to pay them the wage they earn now."

Rachel pressed her eyebrows together. "Do you think that's true?"

Papa shrugged his shoulders. "I don't know. Some people think he is planning to electrify the streetcars, and that will cost a lot of money."

"Electric streetcars?" Sam asked excitedly. "No horses?"

Papa nodded. "It will happen before much longer, I'm sure." He sat down on a sofa.

"I remember when we all went downtown to see the first electric lights on Washington Avenue," Sam said.

Mama chuckled. "You were only five years old. Cousin Seth was sure he had explained everything so that you could understand."

"So if Thomas Lowry pays a higher wage now," Sam said, thinking aloud, "then he won't be able to afford to electrify the streetcar system."

Papa nodded. "I think that's right."

"Electric streetcars will be good for Minneapolis," Rachel said.

"But what about the drivers?" Sam protested. "Is it fair to make their families suffer so we can ride electric cars?"

"What's a strike?" Carrie asked, snuggling next to her father on the sofa.

Papa looked down at Carrie. "A strike would mean that the drivers would tell Mr. Lowry that they won't drive the streetcars."

"Would they get paid if they did that?"

Papa shook his head. "No, if they don't work, they don't get paid."

Carrie was puzzled. "Then they won't get any money. Isn't that worse than not getting a raise?"

Papa laughed. "Now you sound like Uncle Ernest."

"I do?"

"Yes, he says that Mr. Lowry is just making a good business decision. He doesn't force anyone to work for his company. If they don't like the wages, they can look for jobs somewhere else."

"They could work at the flour mills," Rachel suggested.

"A lot of people want to work at the mills," Sam said. "It would be hard to get a job there."

"That's exactly what Mr. Lowry thinks," Papa said. "He believes the drivers need their jobs. Not many of them can afford to go without being paid, and he says they won't find better jobs somewhere else."

"Even if they get other jobs," Mama said, "they might have the same problems."

"You're right," Papa added. "Already there have been two hundred strikes in Minnesota in the last ten years."

"But a streetcar strike will hurt a lot of people besides Mr. Lowry," Sam said. "That doesn't seem fair."

Carrie sat up straight and sniffed the air. "What's that smell?"

"My stew!" Rachel leaped up and flew to the kitchen. She snatched a spoon off the counter and stirred the contents of the pot quickly. The stew was just beginning to stick to the bottom of the pot, but it was not ruined. Thanks to Carrie's sensitive nose, supper was saved. Rachel sighed in relief. She would have to concentrate better than this, or Mama would not let her cook anymore. She stuck a fork in a potato and decided that the vegetables were tender. The peas, which she added now, would take only a few minutes to cook. It was time to bake the biscuits. Rachel was just putting the pan of biscuits in the oven when the rest of her family trailed into the kitchen.

"I told you I don't like burned stew," Sam said.

"It's not burned," Rachel assured him.

"You're not going to burn the biscuits, too, are you?" Sam asked.

Rachel made a face at him. But she glanced at the oven. She had never made biscuits all by herself before. She wanted them to be perfect.

"Can I have butter on my biscuits?" Carrie asked.

"Of course," Mama said. "Why don't you get the butter out and put it on the table?"

Mama had left the stack of bowls on the table. She resumed getting the table ready for the meal.

"Sam, we still need spoons for the stew," Mama said.

Papa sat down in his usual chair.

"I had lunch with Stanley today," he remarked.

"How are the Browns?" Mama asked brightly.

"They are doing well. Miranda is applying for a job at the Boston Clothing Store on Washington Avenue."

Mama chuckled. "She has loved that store from the time she was two. She would do a wonderful job working there."

"That's what Stanley thinks. Freddy is having a hard time settling down in school. His teacher has been sending notes home quite frequently."

Mama smiled. "Well, he is only seven years old. Even Carrie still has a hard time sitting still all day."

"The Browns are fine," Papa said. "But all this business about the streetcars is taking its toll."

"What do you mean?" Sam asked.

Rachel checked the biscuits and stirred the stew. All the while, she listened to what her father had to say.

"Stanley is barely talking to Ernest," Papa said.

"But Ernest is his sister's husband," Mama said. "How can he not talk to them?"

"Oh, he'll talk to Linda. I don't think anything can come between Stanley and Linda. And of course Seth and Miranda are still the best of friends."

"Those two cousins have always been inseparable," Mama said.

Papa frowned. "It's just that Stanley finds it difficult to be around Ernest."

"Stanley and Ernest have always been able to see past their differences before," Mama said.

Papa shook his head. "This is different. Stanley didn't even want to hear me say Ernest's name."

"Is Uncle Stanley mad at Uncle Ernest?" Carrie asked.

"Let's just say they have a difference of opinion," Papa said. "They're having trouble understanding each other."

"What do the streetcars have to do with them?" Rachel asked. Carefully, she lifted the pot of stew from the stove and set it on the table.

"Stanley thinks that the streetcar drivers have a right to form a union and go on strike," Papa answered Rachel. "It's not only the question of higher wages. They also complain that the cars are too open to the elements. They have no protection against the rain, the wind, or the cold."

"And what does Uncle Ernest think?" Sam asked.

"Ernest thinks Thomas Lowry is a good businessman and makes decisions that are good for his company. And Ernest thinks Mr. Lowry has a right to do that. If the street railway company can't make enough money, all the drivers will lose their jobs."

"So maybe it's better if the drivers don't get a raise," Rachel said. "That's better than no job at all."

"But doesn't Uncle Ernest think the streetcar company should be fair to the drivers?" Sam asked.

"What if he can't be fair to the drivers and stay in business at the same time?" Papa countered.

"There must be another way to save money."

"Electric streetcars will be cheaper—once Mr. Lowry can afford to buy them and put in the electrical lines."

"Uncle Stanley and Uncle Ernest don't work for the streetcar company," Rachel said. "Why would they quarrel over this?"

"I asked myself the same thing," Papa said. "But Stanley is part of the railroad union, so he has a lot of sympathy for the streetcar drivers and their union."

"And Ernest is a banker," Mama said, "so he has sympathy for the businesspeople."

Rachel nervously took the biscuits out of the oven. Then she sighed in relief. They were a perfect golden brown and had fluffed up nicely.

"Those look absolutely beautiful, Rachel!" Mama said. "I should have let you make biscuits a long time ago."

"I'll put them in a basket," Rachel said, her pride showing in her blue eyes.

Mama put a ladle in the pot of stew on the table, and the family took their seats. Bowing her head, Rachel listened as her father thanked God for the food. Silently, she added her own prayer: *Please, God, help Uncle Stanley and Uncle Ernest be friends again.*

CHAPTER 2
Who's Right?

"Are you playing baseball today?" Rachel asked Sam the next morning.

"Yep. As soon as I'm done here." Sam pulled the broom across the linoleum kitchen floor as rapidly as he could.

"What else does Mama want you to do?" Rachel was folding laundry on the kitchen table. She had just brought it in from the clothesline in the backyard.

"Nothing. This is my last chore for the day."

"Is it a practice or a game?" Rachel asked, smoothing out one of her cotton skirts.

"Practice. We're getting ready for a game against the Seventh Street team next week." Sam parked the broom in the corner of the kitchen.

"I hope you hit a home run."

"Thanks. I'll be glad just to get a hit." A few minutes later, Sam was off to the baseball field with his bat propped on his shoulder.

After her brother left and Rachel finished the laundry, she got ready for her friends Janie Lawrence and Colleen Ryan. Janie and Colleen liked to cook as much as Rachel did, and the girls were going to look through recipes.

Rachel, Colleen, and Janie had been friends since they were five years old. They had played with dolls together, and now they were learning to cook together. Colleen was happy-go-lucky and always seemed to have a smile on her face. She liked to eat almost as much

15

as she liked to cook. Janie was more serious. Her mother had been ill, so she had learned to cook in order to help out at home. Rachel liked learning to cook with both her friends.

Rachel pulled a plate from the cabinet and took out the jar of cookies that her mother had helped her make the day before. She put a pretty napkin on the plate and carefully arranged the cookies on the plate. She took three glasses from the cabinet so they could have milk with their cookies.

Just as she was going to go pick some flowers from her mother's garden, Rachel heard a knock at the door. When she opened it, her friends were standing there, but they did not sound very much like friends.

"Who says I don't know what I'm talking about?" Colleen said strongly. Rachel had never heard her jolly friend sound so intense.

"If you knew what you were talking about, you wouldn't say the things you are saying," Janie retorted.

"Haven't you heard of free speech? I can say whatever I want to." Colleen nodded to Rachel and pushed past Janie into the house. Janie followed, barely acknowledging Rachel's presence.

Rachel closed the door and looked at her friends. This was so unlike them, and she really did not know what to do. "Uh, what's wrong? Did something happen?" Colleen and Janie just looked at each other.

After what seemed to Rachel like hours, Janie walked over and handed her some papers she had brought. Rachel could see they were recipes that Janie had written out so carefully. Janie headed for the door.

"Janie!" Rachel called. "Aren't you going to stay? Aren't we going through recipes?"

Janie sighed. "I want to, but I don't know if I can." She looked over at Colleen, who was just standing in the middle of the room, arms folded across her chest. Colleen looked away.

Finally, Rachel could stand it no longer.

"What's the matter?" Rachel asked.

"Aw, nothing," Colleen snarled. "Just go look through your recipes."

"It's not nothing," Janie insisted.

"Then what is it?" Rachel asked again. "You're not acting like it's nothing."

"Janie's father works for the streetcar company," Colleen answered.

"I know," Rachel replied. "I've ridden in his car lots of times."

"The union is going to ask for a raise," Janie said. "My father deserves a better wage. He works hard."

"I know he works hard," Rachel said. "Sometimes it's cold and wet in those cars. And the drivers spend all day out in the weather, no matter how bad it is."

"And he works long hours. He's never home for supper. We hardly see him before we go to bed at night."

"I still don't understand what you two are arguing about," Rachel said.

Janie spoke up quickly. "Colleen doesn't want to admit that people like my father deserve to be paid for their work."

"He gets paid," Colleen muttered. "If he doesn't like his wage, he can find a new job. My father says that the streetcar drivers formed a union so they could bully the owners of the company."

"That's not true!" Janie replied. She moved closer to Rachel. "Unions protect the workers. When people stand together, they can do more than when they are alone."

"That's a good point," Rachel said. "It's like Sam's team. They all need each other, or they will never be able to beat that Seventh Street team. Let's go. I have cookies in the kitchen."

Rachel moved toward the kitchen. Neither Colleen nor Janie showed any sign of moving.

Rachel took a mental inventory of her friends. Colleen's father worked at the bank where Uncle Ernest worked. They lived in a nice house, and Colleen always had time to play once her chores were done. Janie's father was a streetcar driver who had to work longer hours to help cover his wife's medical expenses. Free time for Janie, like this morning, was rare. She had to spend a lot of time working around the house and helping to care for her family.

The girls hardly ever talked about what their parents did for a living. Somehow it had never mattered before. They had been together ever since they started school. They all lived within a few blocks of each other. Why should they worry about how their parents made a living? They had all ridden in the streetcar that Janie Lawrence's father drove. When they did, they enjoyed calling the driver by name. They were riding with a friend. *Why should that change,* Rachel wondered, *just because of a union?*

Rachel always looked forward to any time that she could be with her friends—but not because she wanted to listen to a dispute about unions. She wanted to have cookies with her friends and look through recipes. She remembered what her father had said the night before about her uncle Stanley and uncle Ernest.

"Let's do what we came here to do," Rachel said. She hurried past Janie and Colleen and went into the kitchen.

But Janie was not ready. "Unions are not a game," Janie said. "And Thomas Lowry, the owner of the streetcar company, is not interested in families. He just wants to make money."

"He has to run a good business," Colleen said, "or the whole company will go broke. Then no one has a job."

"He doesn't have to make himself filthy rich at the expense of all the drivers."

"Is that what your father says?"

"Yeah."

"He's just jealous of Thomas Lowry."

"That's the nuttiest idea I've ever heard."

Rachel stepped back into the living room. At first Janie and Colleen were both making good points. But now they were sniping at each other. And why did they have to discuss this now, when they were supposed to be having fun doing something they all liked?

"Come on," Rachel pleaded. "Let's go. We're wasting the whole morning."

"Yeah, you're right." Colleen walked into the kitchen and stopped in front of Janie. "I see those cookies. Let's go."

"Oh, okay. Mother was feeling better this morning, so I could come, but I don't want to stay too late. Let's not waste any more time." Janie looked reluctant, but she joined the other girls in the kitchen.

"Let's get started." Rachel put her arms around the shoulders of her friends. She put Janie's recipes on the table, and Colleen added hers to the collection.

"There's milk to go with the cookies. Janie, can you get it? I've got to go get my recipes." Rachel left the girls in the kitchen as she went to her room to get the recipes she had collected from her mother and grandmother.

Rachel was surprised that she did not hear a sound as she came back toward the kitchen. One of the things she had always been able to count on was having a good time with her friends. Yet today no familiar laughter came from the kitchen. No talking, either. With dread, she entered the kitchen. Colleen and Janie were sitting at the table just staring at each other. The milk was still in the pitcher, and the cookies hadn't been touched.

Janie slid her chair back and stood up. "I'd really better leave. I—um—don't like leaving my mother for very long." She picked up her papers and started to leave.

Quickly, Colleen picked up her recipes. "Oh, I forgot. I have plans with my family. How could I have forgotten? We'll have to get together some other time."

Colleen followed Janie to the front door. Slowly, Rachel joined them. "I wish you didn't have to leave," she said as she opened the door. "Please, can't you stay longer?" Both her friends shook their heads no and started down the sidewalk, Janie a few paces ahead of Colleen.

Rachel closed the door and returned to the kitchen. She sat at the table and looked at the plate of cookies she had so carefully prepared. She poured herself a glass of milk and took a cookie. Rachel leaned her chin on her hand. This was supposed to be a wonderful day—just three friends spending time together doing something they loved. What had gone so wrong? Would their friendship survive?

CHAPTER 3
A Friendship Ends

Monday morning came too soon. All day Sunday, Rachel wondered about Janie and Colleen. How long could they stay mad at each other? Neither of them could change what was happening in the streetcar company. But they could play together, just as they had since they were five years old. Rachel had dreaded Monday morning, when she would have to go to school and see Colleen and Janie.

Mama believed in observing the Sabbath. After church on Sunday, she liked the family to spend the afternoon together in quiet activities. Rachel usually read a book. She was in the middle of *Twenty Thousand Leagues under the Sea,* a Jules Verne novel. Her cousin Miranda had recommended the book to her. But even the fantastic imagination of a science fiction writer like Jules Verne could not distract Rachel. All day she wondered how Janie and Colleen could go from being best friends to enemies. Had they ever really liked each other—the way Rachel liked both of them?

Now Monday morning had come. Rachel and Sam entered the school yard. Rachel was further behind Sam than usual. She had a very small build and short legs, and she nearly always had trouble keeping up with Sam's long stride. Today she was having even more difficulty keeping up with him. With his book bag over one shoulder, he turned to look at his sister.

"Don't you feel well, Rachel?" he asked.

"I feel fine," she muttered.

"You look fine, too," Sam observed. "But you're not acting fine. What's the matter?"

"Nothing."

"I don't believe that for a minute. You've been acting strangely ever since Saturday."

"What do you mean?"

"For one thing, you sat still all the way through church yesterday, even when we sang that hymn that you think has such a funny tune."

Rachel shrugged. "So what?"

"So, I think something's wrong. Something happened with your friends. That's when it started."

Rachel gave in. She knew Sam would keep after her until she told him what was wrong.

"Janie and Colleen had a fight," Rachel said. "It's about the unions. They were so mad at each other that they didn't want to go through recipes."

Sam glanced across the school yard. "Here comes Janie now. Colleen is right behind her, but they're not talking to each other."

"See what I mean? They've been best friends since they were little, and now they don't want to talk to each other."

"It doesn't make sense." Sam sighed.

Rachel shifted her attention to another corner of the school yard. "Who is that new girl over there?"

Sam followed her gaze to a girl Rachel's age who sat timidly on a bench alone. "Oh, that's Annalina Borg. Her family just came from Sweden."

"How do you know them?" Rachel asked.

"Uncle Stanley told me about them. Mr. Borg was looking for a job. Uncle Stanley wanted to hire him, but he doesn't have any openings right now."

"So did Mr. Borg find another job?"

Sam shook his head. "I don't think so. But Uncle Stanley says that Mr. Borg wants Annalina to start right out getting an education. He made sure she would start school right away."

"I'll have to be sure to talk to her."

"Good luck." Sam chuckled. "She doesn't speak English."

"Not any?"

"No. They just arrived from Sweden last week."

"She's probably lonely, then. There aren't any other Swedish children in our school."

"Most of them don't live around here. But the Borgs are renting a house in the neighborhood until they find someplace to settle down."

A door on the front of the school opened, and a teacher came out. She pulled vigorously on the rope that moved the brass bell atop the building. The bell clanked, instantly commanding the attention of every student in the schoolyard.

Sam laughed. "There's your teacher. Miss Whittlesey means business today."

Rachel groaned. "She'll probably give us a math quiz."

"I'm glad I'm not in your class."

Inside the school door, Sam and Rachel separated. There were four different classes in the small building, covering eight grades. Rachel walked down the hall to her classroom. Standing at the back of the classroom, she wished she could choose a new seat. Miss Whittlesey had assigned her a seat behind Janie and across the aisle from Colleen. When the assignments were made, all three girls had been ecstatic. Now, Rachel knew, Colleen and Janie would feel differently. Reluctantly, Rachel took her seat. Janie came in and sat in front of her.

"Hi, Rachel."

"Hi, Janie."

Colleen was already sitting across the aisle. Janie did not say a word to her. But Rachel could not ignore Colleen.

"Good morning, Colleen," she said.

"Morning," Colleen muttered without looking up from her desk.

Miss Whittlesey had threatened to give a math quiz, but she didn't. Rachel was relieved. She was not sure she would be able to concentrate well enough to take a test, and she dreaded the thought of what might happen between Colleen and Janie during lunch.

Rachel spotted the new girl at the other side of her classroom, but there was no way to talk with her. Finally lunchtime came. The students burst out the doors of the school with their lunch buckets and scattered around the school yard to enjoy the April spring day.

Rachel was one of the last ones out of the building. She looked around, hoping to talk to Annalina—or at least try to. At last she spotted the fair-headed girl sitting on a bench on the far side of the school yard, unpacking her meager lunch.

Rachel approached her. "Hello," she said brightly.

Annalina looked up, confused. Finally, she forced a smile.

"I know you don't speak English," Rachel said, "but I want to be your friend."

Annalina wrinkled her forehead in concentration. Rachel knew she had not understood anything.

"You have to learn English," Rachel said, "or you won't be able to learn anything else at school."

"English?" Annalina said, finally recognizing a word.

"Yes, English. You must learn." Rachel sat down on the bench next to Annalina. "When my little sister was learning to talk, my mother said that the most important thing was that we all talk to her a lot. So that's what I'm going to do with you. I'm just going to talk until you understand."

Rachel smiled at Annalina, who smiled back blankly.

"I can't imagine what it must be like not to understand anything around you," Rachel said, as she unwrapped her sandwich. "But it can't be very pleasant. You're going to have to learn very quickly, because you don't want to be miserable forever."

Rachel peeled her sandwich apart and held up a slice of Mama's fresh bread. "Bread," she said slowly and distinctly. "Bread."

Annalina looked at the lunch in her lap. She had fruit and a sausage.

"No, you don't have any bread," Rachel said. "But you know what bread is. Just say the word." And she dangled the bread in front of Annalina once more.

"Brud?" Annalina said timidly.

Rachel was careful not to laugh. "Almost. Try again. Bread." She spoke as distinctly as she could.

"Bruad," Annalina croaked.

"That's better," Rachel said. "You just have to practice. Bread."

"Bruad. Bruad. Brrread."

"There you go!" Now Rachel pointed at the fruit in Annalina's lap. "Apple."

Annalina picked up the sausage and said, "Uppa."

"No, that one," Rachel said, pointing again. This time she had her finger nearly on the fruit. "Apple."

Annalina picked up the apple. "Appo?"

"Apple."

Rachel repeated the word as many times as Annalina needed to hear it before she could say it correctly.

"Eat," Rachel said, and she took a bite of her bread.

"Eat," Annalina echoed perfectly.

"That's an easy word, isn't it?" Rachel said. "There are lots of easy words. Maybe we should learn those first."

Annalina smiled and bit her apple. Rachel thought it was a true smile.

In between bites of her own lunch, Rachel continued talking.

"Is our teacher helping you at all?" she asked. "I suppose Miss Whittlesey knows that you don't speak English. But she has so many other students that she won't have time to teach you any words. That's all right, because I can do it. I'll have to find out where you live, though. We won't see each other enough at school."

Annalina smiled again. Rachel could see the anxiety in her blue eyes.

"You have no idea what I'm saying," Rachel said, "but I hope you know that I'm trying to be your friend." She reached out and touched Annalina's blond braid hanging over one shoulder. "I've always wondered what I might look like with braided hair. My mother says I have such beautiful hair that I shouldn't tie it up in knots. But I think you look very pretty."

Rachel twisted the ends of her own hair between her fingers. She and Annalina both had blond hair and blue eyes.

"Hair," Rachel said.

"Eeaare," Annalina croaked.

"Hair." Again Rachel repeated the word as many times as Annalina needed. She glanced across the school yard at Sam. "I wonder if you have any brothers."

Sam had settled under a tree by himself with his lunch. He could feel tension between his friends Jim Harrison and Simon Jones. They had acted kind of strange at baseball practice, as though they suddenly didn't like each other. Sam could see Jim coming toward him. He glanced around. Simon was off to one side, gently tossing a baseball between his hands.

"Hi, Sam," Jim said. "Are you finished eating?"

"Almost."

"We still have a few minutes before the bell rings. How about playing catch?"

Sam hesitated. Out of the corner of his eye, he saw Simon looking in his direction. What would Simon think if he tossed a ball with Jim? Sam was beginning to feel pulled between his two friends.

"I think I need to let my lunch settle," Sam finally said.

"Come on, Sam, just a few throws?"

"Maybe later." Sam stuffed a piece of cheese in his mouth and tried to look busy eating.

Jim shuffled off. But as soon as he was gone, Simon made a beeline for Sam.

"What did Jim want?" Simon demanded.

"He just wanted to play catch," Sam answered.

"But you didn't want to play with him, did you?"

Sam shrugged. "I said I wasn't finished eating."

Simon bent over and looked in Sam's lunch bucket. "It looks like you're finished now. Let's find a bat and hit a few balls."

Sam's stomach sank. He'd been afraid Simon was going to say that.

"Like I told Jim," Sam said, "I want to let my lunch settle."

"You never wanted your lunch to settle before," countered Simon. "You don't even like to eat lunch."

"Well, today I ate lunch, and I want it to settle."

"You're ignoring me, just like Jim. Are you on his side?"

"What are you talking about? What is going on between you two? I noticed it at practice. Simon, you almost hit Jim in the head with a baseball!"

Simon looked at Sam in disbelief. "How can you not know what is going on? Jim thinks the streetcar drivers should go on strike. That's just stupid. Why, Mr. Lowry will go out of business if he has to pay the drivers more. They get paid. If they don't like it, they can go get another job. They can work for Mr. Pillsbury."

Sam shrugged. This was the same thing that had caused the problems between Rachel's friends Colleen and Janie. And between Uncle Ernest and Uncle Stanley. It seemed as though everyone was taking sides.

"So, whose side are you on—mine or Jim's?" Simon prodded.

"I'm not on anybody's side," Sam said. "I just want to eat my lunch."

Across the school yard, Rachel saw the frustration rising in her brother's face. She wondered what Jim and Simon had said to Sam. She could see his tension in the way he held his head. Jim and Simon and Sam had been friends for a long time—just like she and Colleen and Janie.

"Don't worry," she said aloud to Annalina. "We'll be friends because we want to be. None of this other business will matter."

Annalina nodded seriously as if she understood. Knowing she did not, Rachel smiled.

As usual, Rachel was one of the last students out of the building when school was over. Sam hurried to catch up with his sister.

"Sam, what was going on with you, Jim, and Simon at lunch? I saw them talking to you."

Sam looked at Rachel and sighed. "It's the same thing as what's going on between Colleen and Janie—the unions. Jim thinks the streetcar drivers should go on strike, and Simon thinks they shouldn't. I guess it started at baseball practice, but I ignored it and just practiced. Now they want me to choose between them. I just want to be friends—with both of them."

Rachel smiled and nodded at Sam. She knew exactly how he felt. When did being friends and having things in common stop being enough? When did it start to matter whether their fathers were in unions or not?

CHAPTER 4

On Strike

"Why didn't you call me when you were ready to start cooking?" Rachel lifted the lid on one pot to see what Mama was fixing. "I would have come to help you."

"You were doing homework," Mama answered. "I don't like to interrupt you when you're studying."

"I would rather cook."

"Studying is important. You can slice some cheese to have with the soup."

Rachel opened the icebox and removed a chunk of cheddar cheese. Picking up a knife, she asked, "Mama, do you know any Swedish words?"

"Swedish?" Mama was puzzled.

"Don't you have any Swedish friends?"

"Well, yes, I know a couple of Swedish women at church, but they've been in Minneapolis for several years. They speak English."

"Don't you ever hear them speaking Swedish to each other?"

"Sometimes they do. I never paid much attention to what they were saying. Why are you suddenly so interested in Swedish?"

"There's a new girl at school. She's in my class, and she doesn't speak any English."

Mama smiled. "Are you going to try to teach her English?"

Rachel nodded. "She seems like a very nice girl. I sit with her at lunch some days. But I wish I knew a few words that she could understand."

"Why don't you ask her?"

"What do you mean?"

"When you teach her the English word for something, find out the Swedish word."

Rachel thought about her mother's suggestion. "I should have thought of that. I've been too busy teaching her to pronounce 'sandwich.'"

Sam appeared at the back door off the kitchen.

"Oh, good," he said, pulling the door open and dropping his book bag to the floor. "You haven't served supper yet. I was afraid I was late."

Mama glanced at the clock. "As a matter of fact, you are late—very late. But so is your father. I've been waiting for him." She picked up a wooden spoon and stirred the bean soup.

"Is it sticking to the bottom?" Rachel asked.

"It's starting to. If he doesn't come home soon, we'll have to start without him."

"Oh, no, let's wait," Rachel pleaded. "I like it when we all eat together."

"I don't want to eat burned food," Sam said.

"You won't." Rachel stirred the soup some more.

Carrie came in from the dining room. "I'm hungry," she grumbled. "When will supper be ready?"

"It's ready now," Sam said.

"Good." Carrie climbed into a chair. "Let's eat."

"We're waiting for Papa," Rachel said.

"Do we have to?" Carrie whined. "I'm *sooo* hungry."

Mama glanced at the clock again. "I don't understand why he didn't telephone if he was going to be this late."

"That is strange," Sam agreed.

"Maybe there was an emergency," Rachel suggested.

"Yes, I suppose so," Mama murmured.

For another ten minutes, they stirred the pot of soup and speculated about why Papa was so late.

"I'm starving to death!" Carrie declared dramatically. "We can save some food for Papa. Please, let's eat."

Mama sighed and glanced at the clock once more.

"I suppose we might as well," she said. She reached for a stack of bowls and started dishing up the soup.

Carrie carried hers to the table and picked up her spoon.

"Wait until we give thanks," Mama said.

Carrie sighed and put down her spoon.

A few minutes later, Mama, Rachel, Sam, and Carrie sat before their steaming bowls of navy bean soup with bread, meat, and cheese on the platter in the middle of the table. Mama gave thanks to God for the food. Rachel prayed silently that Papa would be safe.

"Finally!" Carrie said, as she plunged her spoon into her soup and slurped up the first mouthful.

Just then the back door opened.

"Papa!" Rachel cried.

"Donald, are you all right?" Mama asked. She rose to her feet to greet him.

Papa kissed Mama's cheek. "I'm sorry I didn't call," he said. "By the time I realized I should call, I wasn't anywhere near a phone."

"You look exhausted," Rachel said.

"What happened, Papa?" Sam asked.

Papa took off his coat and hung it over the back of a kitchen chair.

"Just let me get settled, and I'll tell you all the whole story," Papa said.

Mama dished up Papa's soup, and they all sat down again.

Papa took a bite of bread and then began his story.

"I was so busy today that I hardly noticed what was going on downtown," he said. "I saw nearly two dozen patients at the clinic this morning. Then, after lunch, I went over to the hospital to make my rounds. I thought it was odd that there were no streetcars around. But I didn't have far to go, so I paid no attention. Later, another doctor told me that Thomas Lowry had announced a cut in the wages of the streetcar drivers—two cents an hour!"

"But the drivers already make so little money," Sam said. He thought of Jim Harrison and wondered how his friend would take the news. Rachel worried about how Janie Lawrence's family would get along with a cut in her father's wages. Rachel and Sam glanced at each other, their concern evident in their eyes.

Papa nodded. "I know. I knew Mr. Lowry would not want to give the drivers the raise they wanted. But I did not think he would cut their wages even lower."

"What will the drivers do now?" Rachel passed the platter of meat and cheese to her father.

"They won't drive the streetcars, that's for sure," Papa said. "They went on strike." He took a bite of the cheese Rachel had sliced.

"Strike?" Carrie asked.

"Yes, a strike. The drivers refuse to drive until Mr. Lowry gives back their wages."

"So that's why there were no streetcars when you went out," Mama said.

Papa nodded. "As word spread around the city, the drivers turned back to the car barns. They stabled the horses and hung up their reins. By the middle of the afternoon, no streetcars were running anywhere in the city."

"None at all?" Sam asked.

Papa shook his head. "None."

"But there are over two hundred streetcars."

"Not today. Not even one."

"It's hard to imagine Minneapolis without streetcars," Rachel said.

"We'll all have to get used to it," Papa said. "I don't think this will be settled easily." He chewed on his cheese. "Of course, I didn't realize when I left the hospital that the streetcars weren't running. When I set out for home, I thought I would pick one up along the way. As I said, by the time I realized there were no streetcars, I was far from a telephone. I had no choice but to walk the rest of the way home."

"It's a long way," Mama said. "No wonder it took you so long."

"At least I wasn't alone." He folded a piece of bread around a chunk of cheese. "Everyone who works downtown was in the same situation. We all had to walk."

"What about Uncle Ernest?" Rachel asked. "He has a lame leg. It's hard for him to walk that far."

"I thought of him," Papa said.

"Did you see him leaving the bank?"

"No, I didn't see him. And there was nothing I could do for him anyway. We don't own a carriage."

"No," Mama said. "We've always depended on the streetcars."

"Uncle Ernest doesn't have a carriage, either," Rachel said. "How will he get to work every day without the streetcars?"

Papa shrugged. "I'm not sure what Ernest will do. But I know he thinks Mr. Lowry did the right thing."

"Perhaps we should think about getting a carriage and a horse of our own," Mama said.

"Surely the strike will be settled soon," Sam said.

Papa shook his head again. "I wouldn't count on that. As I walked home, I listened to what people were saying in the streets. Mr. Lowry is a very stubborn man. No one believes he will negotiate with the drivers. Either they do things his way, or they don't work."

"But that's not fair," Sam said. "He should at least talk to the drivers. Maybe if they understood each other better, they would figure something out that would make both sides happy."

"That's not likely."

Rachel and Sam had stopped eating. Only Carrie continued to happily slurp her way through the meal.

"What will happen now?" Sam asked.

Papa sighed. "I'm not sure. I don't think anyone can say. Mr. Lowry might hire other men to drive the streetcars."

"Can he do that?"

"Yes, he can. It's his company. He doesn't have to do what the union tells him to do."

"That doesn't seem fair to the drivers," Sam said.

"Mr. Lowry is not concerned about the drivers. His concern is for his company."

"But the drivers are his company," Rachel said emphatically.

"He doesn't see it that way," Papa said. "His income comes from the passengers. He has to keep the cars running, or he won't make any money at all."

"If he gave the drivers their wages back, he wouldn't have any trouble keeping the cars running," Mama reasoned.

Papa shook his head. "I don't think he will do that."

Sam twirled his spoon in his soup and stared absently at the bread platter.

"Sam, Rachel, you must eat," Mama prodded.

"I've lost my appetite." Sam put his spoon down.

"You must eat anyway," Mama said. "I know this strike will upset a lot of people, but that's no reason to starve yourself."

"Papa," Sam said, "did you happen to see Mr. Harrison downtown? You know, Jim's father."

"No, Sam, I'm sorry. I didn't see him. He must have gone home earlier in the day."

"Oh."

"You'll see Jim tomorrow at school, won't you?"

Sam nodded.

"You can ask him how his father is."

Sam did not answer. Rachel wondered if he was thinking about what Simon would say to Jim.

"And Janie's father. The Lawrences really need the money." Rachel's father nodded at her.

"Papa, I wonder what Uncle Stanley thinks about all this," Rachel said. "I know he likes the unions. He belongs to one."

"I'm sure he supports the strike," Papa said. "He knows how businesses can take advantage of employees."

"It's not fair," Sam said.

"No, it's not," their father agreed.

"It's not fair of the company to cut the wages of the drivers. But it's not fair for the drivers to go on strike, either."

"What good will the strike do?" Rachel asked. "If Mr. Lowry finds other men to drive the streetcars for less money, how does that help people like the Harrisons or the Lawrences?"

"It doesn't," Sam said. "That's why it's not fair. Nobody is helped. Everybody is hurt."

"It sure seems that way to us," Mama said.

"I can't understand why Mr. Harrison would go on strike," Sam said. "He needs his job. And I think he even likes his job. He's always telling stories and joking with the passengers."

"Oh, I know he likes his job," Papa said. "I've heard him say so. But he's a member of the union. If the union votes to go on strike, then all the members go on strike."

"Even if they don't want to?"

"The strength of the union comes from everyone banding together," Papa explained. "If some of the drivers cooperate with Mr. Lowry, then the rest of the drivers will suffer even more. They have to act together, as if they were one person. That's the only way the union can have any power against the company."

Sam nodded. "I know. I've heard Uncle Stanley explain about unions. But it still doesn't make sense to me. Even if all the union members join together as one big person, they are still not as powerful as Mr. Lowry. He owns the company."

"Yes, but he cannot operate the company without drivers," Papa said.

"So they need each other," Rachel said.

"It just might take awhile before both sides realize how much they need each other."

"I hate to think what this will do to Stanley and Ernest's relationship," Mama said. "Agnes and Linda will be pulling their hair out trying to find ways to make their husbands get along."

Papa sighed heavily and pushed his empty plate away. "Let's just pray that someone finds a solution to the strike very soon."

CHAPTER 5
The Union Prepares

"Come on, Sam," Rachel said urgently. She stood near the front door, ready to go. "Annalina will be waiting. Let's go."

"Tell me again what we're doing," Sam said. He looked up from the book he was reading in the living room after school.

"I told Annalina I would take her downtown. She hasn't even seen Bridge Square yet. And I want to show her the shops."

"But it's getting late. The shops will not be open much longer."

"That's all right because we're not really shopping. We're just looking. But Mama says I can't go alone."

"That's right." Mama glanced up from the newspaper. "I'm not sure you should go at all."

"Aw, Mama!" Rachel grumbled.

"There's an article right here in today's newspaper talking about the strike," Mama said. "A lot of people out on the streets are angry. The police have had to break up several fistfights."

"We'll be careful, Mama," Rachel promised. "I already promised Annalina, and she hasn't got a telephone. I don't want to disappoint her."

"What do you think, Donald?" Mama asked.

Papa put down the business section of the paper and looked at Rachel. "I think," he said slowly, "that Rachel should have talked to us before she made a promise to Annalina."

"Please, Papa," Rachel pleaded.

"I understand your mother's concerns," Papa said. "You will have to be extra careful. Can you promise me that?"

"Yes, yes! We'll be so careful!"

"Donald, are you sure about this?" Mama asked doubtfully.

"They're just children," Papa said. "They're not members of any union. I don't think anyone will bother with them."

"But they could get caught in the middle of something."

"That's why we're sending Sam along," Papa said. "Between the two of them, Sam and Rachel have enough sense to stay out of trouble."

"So we can go?" Rachel asked hopefully.

"Yes, you may go," Papa answered.

Rachel looked at Mama.

"If you insist on going," Mama said, "at least take a jar of preserves to Mrs. Borg."

Outside, Sam and Rachel walked for several blocks.

"This isn't the way to Bridge Square," Sam said after a few minutes.

"I know. But it's the way to Annalina's house."

"How far away does she live?"

"About a mile, I think."

"So we have to walk a mile in the wrong direction?"

"It's not the wrong direction. It's the way to Annalina's house."

"But then we have to walk all the way back again, and then the rest of the way to Bridge Square. And then we have to come all the way back to bring Annalina home. That's going to be at least four miles."

Rachel shrugged. "We have time."

"Under the circumstances, I think Annalina would understand if you did not show up at her house."

"There's no reason to disappoint her," Rachel said with determination. And she walked a little faster.

"If we could ride the streetcar, I wouldn't mind," Sam said.

"Look!" Rachel pointed. "There's a streetcar. And it's going our direction." She put out her hand to hail the driver.

Sam grabbed Rachel's arm and yanked her back from the edge of the street.

"Ow!" she protested.

"What do you think you're doing?" Sam hissed.

"You said you wanted to ride a streetcar. And here's a car now. The driver must not be part of the strike."

"All the drivers are on strike," Sam said emphatically. "This driver is a scab."

"A scab?"

"One of the men Thomas Lowry hired to drive the cars in place of the regular drivers. He makes the new drivers promise not to join a union."

The streetcar rattled closer to them. The driver glanced at them hopefully. Sam pulled Rachel farther away from the road. The car rumbled on.

"No one was riding in the car," Rachel said.

"That's right." Sam nodded.

"But why is Mr. Lowry paying men to drive empty cars?"

"He hopes people will get tired of walking and start riding."

"But you don't think so, do you?" Rachel asked. "Just a few minutes ago, you were wishing you could ride a streetcar, but when you had the chance, you wouldn't get on."

Sam shook his head. "It's not safe. I promised Mama and Papa I would look out for you."

"What would happen if we got on a streetcar?" Rachel asked. "If no one else is in the car, how could we get hurt?"

Sam glanced around. "Do you see those people at the next corner?"

Rachel nodded. One block away stood a woman and three young men who looked like they had nowhere to go.

"If we get on," Sam said, "they'll get on. They'll call the driver names and lecture us all the way downtown about destroying everything the union has worked for."

Rachel looked at her brother. "How do you know all this?"

"I talked to Jim."

"I thought you weren't getting along with Jim."

Sam shrugged. "I have nothing against Jim. I don't understand why he's fighting with Simon, but I'm trying to be friends with both of them."

Rachel nodded. She knew how hard that could be. "So what did Jim tell you?"

"His father is thinking about going back to work, because Jim's mama is worried they won't have enough money to pay to their bills." Sam started walking again. "Besides, it doesn't matter now. There won't be another car along this way for a long time."

It took Sam and Rachel almost an hour to walk to Annalina's house and then retrace their steps to go to Bridge Square. As they approached the downtown area, Annalina's blue eyes lit up with a fresh glow. She raced ahead of Sam and Rachel, her braids bobbing over her shoulders. Every few steps, Annalina glanced over her shoulder to make sure Rachel was behind her, but she could not make herself slow down.

Knowing that Annalina could not understand him, Sam said to Rachel, "I've never seen someone so excited about seeing a bridge."

"Bridge?" Annalina said, repeating the word Rachel had taught her a few days ago.

"We've always lived in Minneapolis," Rachel said. "We've seen the bridges our whole lives. If we visited Sweden, we'd be interested in things that other people think are ordinary."

"I suppose so," Sam muttered.

They were on Hennepin Avenue now, heading for the heart of

downtown Minneapolis. In a few minutes, they would be at Bridge Square. From there they could look at the huge Pillsbury mill across the river. Sam hoped there would be trains on the stone arch bridge that carried Jim Hill's railroad across the surging Mississippi River.

Annalina's blue eyes were bright with excitement. She darted from one shop to another, pointing and questioning with her eyes. Smiling, Rachel answered as many questions as she could.

Suddenly, Rachel stopped and pointed.

"Sam, look! Isn't that Uncle Stanley?"

Sam peered down the street. "Yes, and it looks like Seth is with him."

Rachel quickened her steps. "Let's go say hello."

As they got closer, they saw that Uncle Stanley and his eighteen-year-old nephew, Seth, were not just out for an afternoon stroll. Their hands were full of pamphlets, and they were handing one to every person who passed by.

"What is it?" Rachel asked.

"Union literature," Sam answered. He slowed his steps. "Why don't we just go on by? They look busy."

"Don't be silly," Rachel said. "We can't pretend that we didn't see them."

"They haven't noticed us yet," Sam countered.

Just then, Seth waved a long arm.

"Now they have." Rachel started toward her cousins.

Annalina looked confused, but she followed where Rachel led.

"Hello, Uncle Stanley. Hello, Seth," Rachel said cheerfully. "I would like you to meet my friend Annalina."

"Glad to meet you, Annalina," Uncle Stanley said. "What brings you downtown on this fine afternoon?"

"She doesn't speak English," Sam said.

Seth's eyes widened slightly. "Not at all?"

"Only the words Rachel has taught her."

"Oh, I understand." Uncle Stanley turned to Rachel. "So I'll ask you what has brought you downtown today."

"Annalina just moved to Minneapolis two weeks ago. I wanted to show her around." Rachel gestured toward the stack of papers under her older cousin's arm. "Why are you here?"

"We have a union meeting in a few minutes," Uncle Stanley explained. "We're asking people to come inside and hear a speaker."

"Is it about the strike?" Rachel asked.

Uncle Stanley nodded. "The strike will not be settled if people cannot learn to listen to one another."

"I suppose that's true."

Rachel wondered if Uncle Ernest knew that his son Seth was passing out union literature. Surely Uncle Ernest would not approve. He was already unhappy that Seth had taken a job with the railroad while he got ready to go to college. But Rachel decided not to ask about Uncle Ernest.

"Are there many people in there?" Rachel asked instead, pointing to a brick building.

"There is still room for more." Uncle Stanley reached out and handed a pamphlet to a man passing by.

"We'd better go in soon," Seth said.

"All right," his uncle replied. He handed a pamphlet to Sam. "Here, take this home to your father."

"My father is not a union man."

"But he's not against the union, either," Uncle Stanley said. "He might be interested in what we have to say."

Uncle Stanley and Seth disappeared inside the brick building.

"What does the pamphlet say?" Rachel asked.

Sam turned it over and looked at the front. "Stand together," he read. "The strength of many, the mind of one."

"The strength of many, the mind of one," Rachel repeated. "I like that."

Sam looked up from the paper into his sister's blue eyes.

"Are you thinking what I'm thinking?" Rachel asked.

Sam nodded slowly. "But just for a few minutes. After all, you promised to show Annalina the bridge, and soon it will be time to take her home."

Rachel nodded. "I just want to see what it's like."

Once again, Annalina did not understand what was happening, but she followed where Rachel led—into the brick building.

Inside, they crept down a dark stairwell and came to a set of double doors.

"It must be in there," Sam whispered, peeking through the crack between the two doors. His jaw dropped. "There must be three hundred people in that room."

"Open the door," Rachel urged.

"Are you sure?" Sam asked.

Rachel nodded. Annalina looked from Sam to Rachel and back again.

Sam opened the door, and the three of them slipped into the back of the room.

In the front of the room on a makeshift stage, a man stood on a chair. "The mayor is making promises he can't keep," the man shouted. "He promises to protect the drivers. He threatens to arrest anyone who gets in the way of the smooth operation of the streetcar system."

The crowd booed and rumbled.

"This city does not have enough police officers for the mayor to keep that promise," the man shouted, thrusting his fist in the air. "We have people standing on every corner watching the cars. We know who is riding and who is not."

"See?" Sam whispered. "Isn't that what I told you?"

"Shh!" Rachel wanted to hear more.

The man on the chair continued. "This is not the first strike in Minneapolis, and it will not be the last. Organized labor will grow in strength, grow in numbers, grow in influence."

The crowd cheered. Sam spotted Uncle Stanley in one corner. He was starting to applaud.

"The day of management's power is past," the man said. "We are entering a more humane era. In the future, a man who gives an honest day's work will get an honest day's wage. He will use that wage to care for his family, to bring up his children in dignity."

The crowd roared and chanted, "Stand together, stand together."

Annalina clutched Rachel's arm so tightly it hurt. "What mean?" she said. Her blue eyes had lost their glow and become frightened.

Rachel sighed. "If only I could explain it to you. Your father would understand. It's the same reason he brought you here—the reason he wants you to go to a good school."

Annalina searched Rachel's face with questioning eyes.

"We'd better go," Sam said.

CHAPTER 6

Annalina's Problem

"We sit here?" Annalina asked hopefully.

"Very good!" Rachel exclaimed. "Yes, we'll sit here." With a cotton handkerchief, she dusted off a wooden bench. "Now, I know you've never seen a baseball game before, so I'll try to explain the rules."

Annalina peered at the baseball diamond, with the shapeless white sandbags evenly spaced around it.

"One team will try to hit the ball and run all the way around," Rachel explained. "They have to touch all the bases. The other team will try to stop them. Each team gets three outs, and there are nine innings."

Annalina looked at Rachel, completely confused.

"I never realized how complicated it is to explain baseball." Rachel loved baseball games. "You'll get the idea when they start playing a real game."

Sam had talked for weeks about playing the team from Seventh Street. Apparently many of the other players had, too. Quite a few family members had turned out to watch the match. Rachel was surprised to see some of her friends from school. Some of the girls had brothers on Sam's team. Colleen and Janie were supposed to come with Rachel to the game, until. . .

Rachel turned and waved to a row of girls behind her. No one waved back. Instead, Rachel saw several of them put their heads together. She could tell from the way their shoulders were moving that they were laughing. Katherine Jones glanced up at Rachel. But instead of catching Rachel's eyes, she quickly turned her head back to the huddle.

"Baseball," Annalina said very distinctly. She gestured as if she were throwing a ball.

"Very good," Rachel said. She gestured as if she were swinging a bat and said, "Bat."

"Bat. Bat." Annalina echoed.

Behind them, Rachel heard another echo. She twisted around to see her friend Mariah Webster saying, "Baht, baht. Ja, ja, dis ist baht."

Mariah and Katherine burst into giggles. "Ja, ja."

Rachel stared at Mariah. Mariah stared back.

"Mariah Webster, you stop that!" Rachel demanded.

Mariah and Katherine giggled even harder.

Rachel turned to face the field again, her arms crossed on her chest. "Never mind them," she said to Annalina. "We have a ball game to watch."

Both teams were finishing their warm-ups. Soon it would be time to begin playing. Sam did not seem to be concentrating on the warm-up, however. His eyes were raised to the outfield. Simon had not shown up for the game. Rachel knew Sam must be hoping that Simon was just late. But as the minutes dragged by, Rachel realized that Simon might never come to play on the team again. Simon was their best hurler. Without him throwing the ball, the team could be in for a great deal of trouble on the field.

"I'll be right back," Rachel told Annalina. She made her way between the benches to the edge of the field where she could hear the boys' voices.

"He's not coming, is he?" she heard Steve Jones say to Sam.

Sam shook his head. "I guess not."

"Maybe he's sick," Steve said.

"Naw," said another boy, "I saw him on Bridge Square this morning. He's fine."

"Maybe his parents wouldn't let him play today," Sam speculated. "Maybe they had relatives visiting or something."

"Naw, they come to all the games. More likely they wouldn't let him play because they don't want him on this team anymore."

"That's ridiculous," Sam said. "He's played on this team for three years. They never minded before."

"It's different now."

"No, it's not. It's the same team."

"Now Jim's father and Simon's father are on opposite sides of the strike."

"So what?" Sam said. "That doesn't mean they can't play baseball together."

"Yes, it does." It was Joe Rugierio's turn to speak. "My parents didn't want me to come, either. Most of you are management families."

"We're just families!" Sam insisted. "And we're the same team we've always been."

Rachel sighed and made her way back to her seat beside Annalina. The game should have started by now, but most of Sam's team was still standing around talking. And Simon, the star pitcher, wasn't there. Of all games to miss, this was the big one with the Seventh Street team.

"I'm sure the game will start soon, Annalina," Rachel said. "They're just planning their strategy."

Annalina nodded, but Rachel could tell that she didn't understand. Rachel hunched forward, hoping that the game would start soon.

"Hey!" called the captain of the other team. "Are we going to play ball or what?"

"We're almost ready!" Sam called back. He turned back to his teammates. "So, who is going to hurl today?"

Rachel watched while they chose Larry Lerner to take Simon's place on the pitching mound. They would be short one player in the outfield. They scattered to take their positions.

Rachel leaned on her knees to study the first batter. Her stomach sank as she recognized this batter. Sam's team would not be able to get anything past him.

Larry let the first pitch go. It was so far out of the strike zone that the other team burst into laughter.

"It's okay, Larry, just keep your focus," Sam called out. He clapped his hands in encouragement.

Larry wound up again. The pitch was straight this time, but not very fast. The batter had plenty of time to get a good look at it and swing hard. He whacked the ball right over Sam's head and into left field. Steve Jones scrambled after it. By the time he chased it through the grass and heaved it to the infield, the batter was standing on second base, grinning at Sam.

Larry looked lost. Rachel saw Sam go to the mound to speak to him. She knew he was trying to make Larry feel better.

The second batter came up to the plate. The runner took a generous lead off second base. It was as if he knew what would happen next. Larry only threw one pitch. The batter swung. Rachel groaned. She could tell from the sound that the hit was a home run. The batter whooped his way to first base and then kept going. While the outfielders retrieved the ball, the two players from the Seventh Street Spades trotted around the diamond victoriously. The score was two to nothing, with no outs in the first inning.

Larry walked the next two batters, with eight very wide pitches in a row. Sam crouched in his position. There was still hope for a double play if the batter hit the ball to Joe. Joe could snap the ball to Sam on second, who would throw it to Jim. Rachel knew it could all happen in one smooth motion they had practiced a hundred times. She held her breath.

But the next ball did not come to shortstop. It went to right field. The runner on second base scored easily, and now there were runners on first base and third base—and still no outs. Rachel sighed. Three to nothing. This was going to be a long game. And they were getting killed in the first inning.

She turned to Annalina. "Sam's team is not doing well yet. Three members of the other team have touched all the bases, including home plate. That means they're ahead three to nothing. But, Sam's team hasn't come to bat yet."

Again, Annalina nodded, but Rachel was sure she didn't understand what Rachel was trying to explain to her. As Rachel searched for words to better explain what had happened, she thought she caught a glimpse of Simon standing at the edge of the park. When Rachel looked back, though, Simon was gone.

Rachel turned her attention back to the game. Larry walked another batter. The bases were full. Rachel watched as Sam put his hand up for a time-out. The team gathered on the pitcher's mound. "Just a minute," Rachel whispered to Annalina. She slipped down to the front of the benches again where she could hear what was going on.

"We have to help Larry out here," Sam was saying.

"You mean we have to get him out of there," Joe said.

"That's exactly right." Sam took the ball from Larry and slapped it into Joe's hand. "You're the pitcher now."

"But who's going to play shortstop? What about the double play ball?"

"Look, you're used to throwing at me and hitting the mark in double plays. You have to do the same thing throwing at the plate. Larry can cover second, and I'll play short."

"It seems to me that we need help in the outfield," Steve said. "That's where all the hits are going."

Sam shook his head. "Not anymore, right, Joe? From now on, the ball doesn't leave the infield."

Joe nodded seriously.

"But the bases are full," Steve reminded everyone, "with no outs. We've got to watch the play at the plate."

"Come on," chided the captain of the Seventh Street Spades. "Are you going to play or not?"

The boys on the Spades howled with laughter. "Maybe they're too weak from their desk jobs," one of them said. "Baseball is too much like physical labor. You actually have to move your muscles to play."

"That must be it!" another one scoffed. "They're in no condition to play against a union team."

Joe snapped his head around to Sam. "Are you going to let them get away with saying that?"

"The only thing to do," Sam said calmly, "is to pull ourselves together and prove we're the great team we know we are."

Rachel felt proud of her brother as she made her way back to her seat. Clearly, though, the team was in a lot of trouble. She saw Sam move the ball from Larry to Joe. But she also knew that no one was as good as Simon. They needed Simon more today than they ever had before.

"Hit ball," Annalina said. "Boy hit ball."

"That's right," Rachel said. "We just didn't want so many boys to hit the ball."

"Hit ball," came the snickering voices behind them.

Rachel turned around and glared at Mariah again. Mariah laughed aloud.

"You're sitting with a scab," Mariah said loudly. "Did you know that, Rachel Borland? You're sitting with a scab. I saw her father driving a streetcar yesterday."

Rachel glanced at Annalina. "Is that true, Annalina? Is your father driving a streetcar?"

"Drive? Ja, Papa drive."

So it was true. Mr. Borg was driving one of those empty street-cars rattling around town.

It was all Rachel could do to keep from edging away from Annalina. But it would do no good, and Rachel did not want to hurt Annalina's feelings. She glanced at Annalina's face. Her new friend did not look as excited as she had a few minutes earlier. *She understands,* Rachel thought. *She understands what Mariah is saying and what those other girls are doing.*

The game had to get better. Rachel could not imagine that it could be any worse.

She watched as Joe got ready to throw his first pitch. He took a long time, and he looked over his shoulder at Sam two times. Finally, he threw the ball. It was a good pitch—right into the strike zone. The batter let it pass. But at least Joe Rugierio had thrown the first strike of the game.

Rachel sighed in relief. If only Joe could do that a few more times. Once again, Joe got ready to hurl the ball. Another strike! The Seventh Street team had stopped laughing.

On Joe's third pitch, the batter swung. It was a weak hit and took a long time to dribble to shortstop. Sam fielded it easily, but it was too late to throw it to home plate. He had to settle for throwing the ball to Jim at first base. One run scored, and the other runners advanced. But at least there was one out. The score was four to nothing, with runners on second and third.

The next batter got a good hit. Both runners scored, and the batter ended up on second base. Six to nothing. Then Joe struck out a batter. It took eight pitches, but he did it. Two out.

Rachel just wanted the inning to be over. They were down by six runs, but it was only the first inning. The Spitfires had some good hitters on their team. If they could just get a chance to bat, they might be able to even the score.

Glancing across the field, Rachel was sure she saw Simon leaning against the fence with his hands stuffed in his pockets.

By the time the inning was over, the Seventh Street team led by eight runs. Now Rachel just wanted the game to be over. She was certain Sam must feel the same.

CHAPTER 7
A Fight in the Family

"I'm so glad you stopped by, Linda." Mama poured three cups of tea: one for herself, one for Aunt Linda, and one for Rachel. Mama usually did not include Rachel in the grown-up tea talks. Rachel was going to be on her best behavior so Mama would do it again sometime.

"Easter is just a few days away," Mama said. "We need to make plans for dinner after church."

"It's my turn to have the family over," Aunt Linda said. She dropped a sugar cube into her tea.

"Are you sure?" Mama asked. "I would be happy to have Easter dinner here."

"Nonsense," Aunt Linda said. "You've had the last two birthday parties. Let me do it."

Rachel did not care where Easter dinner would be. But she did care what they would eat and hoped it would be something she could help prepare. Rachel sat down at the kitchen table next to her mother and across from Aunt Linda. Sam was at the end of the table. Mama had not offered him any tea. Rachel knew he would not drink it anyway.

"Can we have that currant glaze on the ham?" Sam asked.

"Do you mean the one that Agnes makes?" Mama asked.

"That's the one. I love that glaze!" Sam smacked his lips.

"I'm sure she will be willing to make the glaze—just for you."

"I'll get the ham, of course," Aunt Linda said, "and the sweet potatoes."

"What will we make, Mama?" Rachel asked.

"What would you like to make?"

"Pies," Rachel answered. "I want to learn to make a good pie crust."

"Ugh!" Sam groaned. "Do you have to experiment on the rest of us?"

"Hush, Sam," Mama said. "Your sister is turning into a fine cook. You should be glad to have her around. I know I am."

Rachel beamed.

"What kind of pies?" Aunt Linda asked.

"Peach, apple, strawberry, cherry." Rachel listed all her favorites.

Mama chuckled. "We'll see what kind of fruit preserves we have in the cellar."

"Can we use Pillsbury's Best flour for the crust?" Rachel asked.

"Of course. How could we live in Minneapolis and not buy the best flour in the country?"

"Where's Ernest?" Mama asked. "Maybe he has some suggestions for the menu."

"He's in the living room going over some papers," Aunt Linda said. "If we ask him what he'd like, the list will be far too long to accomplish."

Mama laughed.

A knock on the front door brought the menu planning to a halt.

"Sam, please go see who that is," Mama said.

He darted off to answer the door. Rachel cocked her ear toward the voices that drifted into the kitchen from the hallway.

"It's the Browns!" Rachel jumped to her feet. "I wonder if Freddy is with them."

Mama glanced at Aunt Linda. "I'm sorry, Linda, I had no idea they would be coming by."

"It's all right. You didn't know Ernest and I would drop in, either. We're all here. I'm sure everything will be fine."

Aunt Agnes appeared in the doorway. Her seven-year-old son

55

Frederick was right behind her.

"Is Stanley with you?" Mama asked.

Aunt Agnes looked over her shoulder nervously. "I left him in the living room with Ernest and Sam."

"Have Ernest and Stanley seen each other lately?"

Aunt Agnes and Aunt Linda both shook their heads emphatically.

"Then they'll have a lot to catch up on," Mama said optimistically.

Rachel was not so sure it was a good idea to leave Uncle Stanley and Uncle Ernest in the same room.

"What do you have to eat?" Freddy demanded.

"Frederick!" his mother scolded.

"I'm sorry. Cousin Dorthea, might I have a bit of a snack?"

Mama smiled. "Such a little gentleman. Of course you may have a snack. Rachel, why don't you see what we have?"

Rachel got up and went to the icebox. "How about leftover chicken?" she suggested.

"White meat or dark?" he asked suspiciously.

"It's a leg."

"Good. I'll take that."

"Freddy," his mother coaxed.

"Thank you, Rachel, I would like the chicken leg."

"We were just discussing Easter dinner," Mama said. "Linda has offered to have everyone at her house. And Sam has put in a request for your currant glaze."

Aunt Agnes sighed and glanced toward the door that led to the living room. "A family dinner would be nice. We haven't done that for a long time."

Rachel put the chicken leg on a plate and set it in front of Freddy. Aunt Agnes had a strange look on her face.

"What is it, Agnes?" Mama asked.

Aunt Agnes hesitated. She glanced at Aunt Linda.

"It's all right," Aunt Linda said. "I can see that you're nervous about Stanley and Ernest being together. To be honest, I am, too."

"I hate to create a situation where they might quarrel," Aunt Agnes said.

"But we can't stop bringing the family together because Stanley and Ernest don't agree on unions and management. Stanley and Ernest have known each other a long time. I believe they are genuinely fond of each other."

"I'm sure they are, too," Aunt Agnes said. "And they both love you, Linda. But lately Stanley is so edgy about this union business. I can't predict how he will behave."

"They seem to be doing just fine right now," Mama said. "You left Stanley in the living room with Ernest, and we haven't heard a peep out of them."

"That's not necessarily good," Aunt Agnes said. "It means they're not speaking to each other at all."

Just then, Sam entered the kitchen. He slumped into a chair. "I'd rather listen to you talk about recipes," he said, "than sit in there with the two of them."

"What's going on?"

"Nothing. That's the problem. They're just sitting there staring at each other. Uncle Ernest pretends to be working on his papers, but I don't think he really is. And Uncle Stanley is making me crazy, jiggling his leg all the time."

"Jiggling his leg?" his wife said in alarm. "That means something is on his mind." She turned to Sam. "Didn't he say anything at all?"

Sam shrugged. "He asked me about my baseball team. But I don't think he heard a word I said."

"Is he twitching his moustache?" Freddy asked, his mouth full of chicken.

Sam nodded.

Freddy and Aunt Agnes looked at each other.

"Papa's going to be angry, isn't he?" Freddy said what they were all thinking.

Just at that moment, the voices in the next room exploded. Rachel's heart raced as she jumped out of her chair. Sam was ahead of her, bounding into the living room. Mama and the other women were right behind them. They stood at the edge of the living room. The men seemed not to notice anyone had entered the room.

"You're an intelligent man, Stanley," Uncle Ernest was saying. "I do not understand why you are behaving like such a simpleton on this matter."

The color was rising in Uncle Stanley's face. "You see the world one way, Ernest, and I see it another way."

"You see the world the way you want to see it," his brother-in-law retorted. "You want the unions to be powerful, so you inflame the average person. You fill their heads with ideas that can never come true."

"The unions will make their ideas come true—and life will be better for the average worker."

Uncle Ernest slapped the table next to his chair. Rachel jumped back.

"When will you understand that the people who own these businesses have something to say on these questions?" he shouted. "You want to create a perfect world for the average worker, but you want the owners to pay for it—men like Charles Pillsbury and Thomas Lowry. They've worked hard to build up their businesses."

"They've made themselves rich by keeping their workers in poverty!" Uncle Stanley stood up and towered over Uncle Ernest.

"Mama?" Rachel whispered. "Shouldn't we do something?"

"I'm not sure what to do," Mama answered.

"Don't do anything," Aunt Linda said. "Stanley and Ernest are grown men. Eventually they have to work this out."

Sam was not convinced. "What if they don't?"

Carrie tumbled down the stairs from her room and ran to her mother. "Mama, why are they yelling?"

Uncle Ernest pushed his papers aside and pulled himself out of his chair. He was not as tall as Stanley, and his cork leg made him unsteady for a moment. But he stared up at his opponent and continued his side of the argument. His jaw was set, and his words were clipped.

"Am I to believe that you think getting no pay at all is better for those workers than the pay Mr. Lowry offers?"

"The wage cut is only part of it. The strikers are standing on a principle, Ernest."

"And their children are going hungry for the sake of that principle," retorted Uncle Ernest. "Does the principle justify the way they terrorize the new drivers or the way they taunt anyone who tries to ride a streetcar?"

"They are doing what they believe they must do."

"And what if they are wrong?"

The front door opened and Papa came in. Instinctively, Rachel flew across the room and snuggled against him.

Papa put down his medical bag next to the door and looked around the living room.

"What in the world is going on in here?" Papa demanded. "I could hear you halfway down the block."

The two men did not answer. They continued to glare at each other.

"Don't bother to answer," Papa said, "because there is no good answer. There is no excuse for the way you two are behaving. I don't care what is going on in the streets, and I don't care what the politicians are saying. You will not bring your arguments into my home."

Uncle Stanley broke his stare and turned to Papa. "I'm sorry, Donald. Of course you are right. We let things get out of hand."

But Papa was not finished. "Stanley, Ernest is married to your sister. I would think that out of respect for Linda, you would make an effort to be civil to him. And you, too, Ernest. Do not forget that Stanley is Linda's brother."

"You are quite right, of course." Uncle Ernest turned around and picked up his papers. "Linda, I believe we should leave now." He moved toward the door without so much as glancing at his brother-in-law.

Rachel watched Aunt Linda's face. Whatever she was thinking or feeling, she did not show anything in her face. Aunt Linda turned to Mama and Aunt Agnes.

"I'll telephone you," she said. "We'll finish making our plans for Easter dinner over the phone."

"Are you sure we should get together?" Aunt Agnes whispered, glancing up at her husband. "It could be very unpleasant."

Linda kept her voice even. "Easter Sunday celebrates the resurrection of our Lord—victory over sin. That includes family arguments. I will not let this union business destroy our family."

"Linda," Uncle Ernest called as he opened the front door.

"Don't forget the glaze, Agnes," Linda said over her shoulder as she headed for the door.

As soon as the couple had gone, Uncle Stanley said, "Agnes, perhaps we ought to be on our way as well. We only meant to stop in for a moment."

"Yes, of course," she replied. "I'll just get Freddy."

In another moment, they were gone as well.

Rachel looked up at Papa. "Will Uncle Stanley and Uncle Ernest be friends again?" she asked. "When the strike is settled, will they stop fighting?"

Papa sighed. "I hope they stop fighting no matter what happens with the strike. They are both bigger and stronger than this petty arguing."

"But they don't think it's petty," Sam said. "They're on opposite sides, and they both think they're right."

"Then we must help them to see the truth," Papa said. "Both Mr. Lowry and the unions have some good arguments. They have to learn to listen to each other—and that includes Ernest and Stanley."

CHAPTER 8

Lost!

"Can we go? Can we go?" Eight-year-old Carrie twirled to make her new pink Easter dress spin.

"What's your hurry?" Sam asked. "Easter dinner is not for two more hours."

"I want to play with Freddy," Carrie said.

"Be careful of your new dress," Mama said. "Perhaps you should take an old frock along to play in later."

"No!" protested Carrie. "I want to keep my new dress on. I've hardly worn it at all—just to church this morning." Carrie twirled around the kitchen. The wide skirt of her new pink cotton dress spun in a perfect circle.

"Everyone looked beautiful in church today," Rachel said. "Cousin Miranda should always wear that color of green. And Molly looked so wonderful sitting next to her beau."

Mama took a pie from the oven and set it on the counter. "Carrie, please stop spinning. You're going to knock something over."

"I'm being careful!" Carrie protested.

Mama warned her with a raised eyebrow, and Carrie screeched to a halt.

Rachel gently touched the top of the pie, testing for doneness.

"Mmm." Sam smacked his lips loudly. "Maybe we should have a snack now."

"Don't you touch my pie!" Rachel said.

"It looks perfect, Rachel," Mama said. "You should be proud of yourself."

Rachel was proud. "Let me wrap it up, Mama." She pulled open a cupboard and reached for a towel. "I want to carry it."

"Mama, is Freddy really going to be there?" Carrie asked.

"Of course he is. The whole family will be there."

"Everyone?"

"Everyone. The Browns, the Stockards, everyone."

"Even Uncle Stanley?"

"Why, of course Stanley will be there."

Carrie stuck her lower lip out thoughtfully. "Freddy's family did not sit in front of us today at church. They always sit in the row in front of us."

Mama started wrapping up a basket of biscuits. "Church was very crowded today because it was Easter. Freddy's family had to find a seat in the back."

"No, they didn't," Carrie said. "They were there early. I saw them. Freddy said his father did not want to sit near Uncle Ernest."

Rachel watched Mama carefully. How would she explain why the two men were angry with each other?

"What else does Freddy say?" Mama asked casually. She laid a linen napkin over the top of the biscuit basket.

"He says that his papa says Uncle Ernest doesn't understand about the streetcar strike. He says Uncle Ernest is being too stubborn for his own good."

Mama nodded. "Yes, that's what Stanley thinks."

"Is he right, Mama?" Carrie seemed to genuinely want to know.

"It's very complicated, Carrie. Why don't we talk about it another time? But I promise you that Freddy will be there today, and you can play with him all afternoon."

"Then let's go!" Carrie cried.

"I believe we are ready." Mama said.

Rachel's stomach was a little nervous. If her two older cousins sat down at the same table, how long would the family dinner last? Aunt Linda had a long table, and there would be fourteen people there— fifteen if Molly brought her new beau. Uncle Stanley and Uncle Ernest would not even have to talk to each other. But would they be able to control themselves? Would they want to?

Mama and Carrie were ready to go.

"Shouldn't we wait for Papa?" Rachel asked.

Mama shook her head. "He had to see a patient at the hospital. I told him just to meet us at the Stockards'."

"I suppose it would be silly for him to come all the way back here first." Rachel buttoned her new sapphire cloak under her neck.

"Especially with no streetcars running," Sam added.

They gathered their things and started out. Rachel carried the cherry pie, while Mama carried the apple pie and corn pudding. Carrie had the biscuits. Sam lugged a sack of potatoes destined to be peeled, boiled, and mashed at the Stockards' house.

As they walked, Carrie chattered about her new dress and the new wooden top she carried in her pocket to show Freddy. Rachel concentrated on keeping the cherry pie level. Even through the thick towel she had wrapped around the pie plate, she could feel the warmth and smell the sweet cherry filling. Her stomach growled.

Sam scanned the neighborhood. "A lot of people are out walking today," he observed. "Most people stay home on Sunday afternoons."

Rachel could see that Sam was right. A lot of people were in the streets. "Maybe they are out for the same reason we are," she said. "Waiting for their Easter dinner."

Sam squeezed his eyebrows together. "I don't think so. They're not carrying food. And most of them are not really walking. They're just standing around."

Once again, Sam was right. Rachel was starting to feel nervous.

"Mama?" she said quietly.

"I'm sure everything is fine," Mama said. "People are a bit restless with the strike, that's all."

Rachel was not convinced. She looked at Sam. He seemed to be watching the street carefully.

"We're walking too slow," Carrie announced, paying no attention to the conversation. She proceeded to skip.

"Carrie," Mama warned. "Don't get too far ahead of me."

"Here comes a streetcar," Carrie said, pointing.

The car was empty, of course. Rachel could see straight through it. The car was headed toward downtown.

"Isn't that Annalina's father?" Sam asked.

"Where?" Rachel's eyes darted through the crowd.

"In the streetcar," Sam said. "I think he was driving."

The car stopped at the next corner, and an elderly woman boarded. Immediately two young men swung aboard. Even from down the block, Rachel could hear them heckling the driver.

"Scab!"

"Management sympathizer!"

The car rumbled down the street. Rachel could see the two young men hovering over the driver. At the next stop, the elderly passenger got off.

"She's an old lady," Sam said, disgusted. "Why don't they leave her alone and let her ride?"

"Do you really think that was Annalina's father?" Rachel asked.

"I didn't get a good look," Sam said, "and I've only seen her father once. But she told you he had started driving streetcars."

"Do you think we could catch up with it?"

"Now, Rachel," Mama said, "I understand your concern about your friend's father. But you cannot put yourself in danger. He made his own choice to drive a streetcar."

"I just want to know if it was him."

The car had stopped again, three blocks up. Rachel peered down the street, trying to focus on the driver's profile.

"Carrie!" Mama called. "Wait for me."

Rachel did not turn around at her mother's voice. Why couldn't Carrie just be patient and walk with the rest of the family?

Try as she might, Rachel could not see the driver clearly. He was too far away.

"I can't see him," she said, disappointed. No one answered her.

Now she whirled around. Where was Mama? And Carrie and Sam?

In the last few minutes, the street had flooded with dozens of people. Where had they all come from? And what were they doing? They seemed to move like the current of the Mississippi River toward downtown Minneapolis. Caught up in the pressure of the growing crowd, Rachel stumbled along for a few feet, clutching her still-warm pie. She examined the crowd for her mother's bright blue shawl or Carrie's new pink dress. They were nowhere to be seen.

"Sam!" she cried aloud. "Mama!" Rachel could feel tears of panic springing to her eyes.

A couple people passing by turned to glance at her. But there was no flicker of recognition in their eyes. They were strangers.

Stay calm, Rachel told herself. *They can't have gone far. You only turned your head for a moment.*

Against her will, Rachel was moving down the street with the flow of the crowd. Cradling her pie, she pressed her way out of the mainstream. Mama always told her that if she got lost, she should stay where she was and someone would find her. She was lost now. Rachel determined to get out of the crowd and stay put.

Rachel pressed herself up against a fence. She recognized the well-tended home before her. It was Mariah Webster's house. The picket at the top of the fence was poking into Rachel's back. But she hardly felt it. She poured all her energy into looking for her family in the throbbing mob.

The murmurs of the crowd had swelled to a roar. Mumblings had become shouts. Rachel could hear what the people were saying.

"We'll teach them a lesson they won't forget!"

"We'll show that Thomas Lowry that he needs us more than he thinks he does."

"We have to get rid of those scabs."

Get rid of the scabs? What do they mean? Rachel wondered.

Three men charged down the middle of the street, shoulder to shoulder, marching in step.

Over the noise of the crowd, Rachel cried out, "Mama! Sam!"

"Rachel!"

Relief swept over Rachel at the sound of her brother's voice.

"I'm here, Sam, here!"

She still could not see him.

"I'm coming!"

And then he was there.

"What happened?" Rachel asked.

Sam shook his head. "I'm not sure. Mama chased after Carrie, and when we turned around, you were gone."

"But I didn't go anywhere!"

"Never mind. I found you."

"But where are Mama and Carrie?"

The crowd around them thickened by the moment. Dozens had turned into hundreds, perhaps even thousands.

"I've never seen so many people," Sam said, "except at the ballpark or a parade."

"Sam, where are Mama and Carrie?" Rachel asked again, more urgently this time.

Sam turned to look at his sister and sighed. "I don't know."

"Are they waiting for you somewhere?"

"I don't know. Mama was worried about you, and I said I would find you. And now—"

"And now it will be impossible to find them."

"Let's not give up yet." Rachel could see the concentration in her brother's dark eyes. "We haven't even started looking yet."

Rachel swallowed a sob. "I never did like crowds."

Still carrying the sack of potatoes, Sam offered his elbow. "Here, hang on to me. Whatever you do, don't let go."

"Believe me, I won't!"

"Let's go back to the corner where you saw the streetcar," Sam suggested. "That's the last place we were all together."

Rachel thought that was a good idea. But it was harder than it sounded. Everyone else was swarming down the street in the other direction. With one hand, she held her prized pie. With the other hand, she squeezed Sam's elbow. Together, they forged their way against the ever-growing stream.

Men of all ages filled the street, and women and children, too. The men marched with determination toward a goal Rachel could not see. The children whooped and hollered. Rachel heard the edge of her new cloak rip when someone pulled on it. She jerked herself away and held onto Sam's arm even more tightly.

"Sam, what are all these people doing?"

"What did you say?" Sam shouted.

"I said, what are all these people doing?"

Sam shook his head in confusion.

"Do you think Mama and Carrie are all right?" Rachel asked anxiously.

They had arrived at the corner where they had seen the streetcar, but there was hardly room to stand there. Hundreds of people flooded the intersection. But Rachel could see no sign of a bright blue shawl or a new pink dress.

"Sam, what if we don't find them?" Rachel said. "Mama always says to stay put when you get lost."

"We can't stay here," Sam said. "Even Mama would say that this is dangerous."

Rachel's heart raced. Where was Mama?

"We have to get out of the way of this mob," Sam said.

"But what about Mama and Carrie?" Rachel pleaded.

Sam hesitated only a moment before answering. "Mama will do whatever she has to do to keep Carrie safe. And she would want us to keep ourselves safe."

Rachel nodded. Sam was right. "But where will we go?"

CHAPTER 9
The Easter Riot

"Come on," Sam said. "This way."

"Where are we going?" Rachel asked.

Sam must not have heard her. He did not answer. Rachel held on to his arm a little tighter. She thought how silly they must look carrying a sack of potatoes and a cherry pie through the mob.

Rachel realized Sam was leading her straight into the heart of the crowd. "What are you doing?" She tugged on his elbow.

Sam shouted over his shoulder, "Trust me!"

Rachel got bumped from the back. The cherry pie started to slide. She jerked her arm from Sam's elbow and gripped the pie more securely with both hands.

Sam turned around to see what had happened. "I told you not to let go of me."

"I'm sorry. The pie started to fall."

"Forget about the pie." Whatever calm Sam had managed to hang on to was disappearing. His dark eyes darted back and forth, alert to every movement of the crowd.

Rachel took Sam's elbow again, but she kept her grip on the pie. They were carried along by the crowd until they came to the next corner. Sam steered them down a side street where they rested.

Rachel swallowed the lump in her throat.

Sam was breathing heavily. "We have to figure out what we're going to do."

Rachel watched the crowd around them and wished she were somewhere else, anywhere else. She kept looking for Mama and Carrie. Everything looked brown and gray. Nothing was blue or pink.

"We should keep going to the Stockards'," Rachel suggested. "Everyone will expect us there."

Sam shook his head. "It's too far—at least another mile."

"But Mama will go there."

"I'm not sure what Mama will do. If she's trapped in the crowd like we are, she won't be able to get to the Stockards' either."

"We could go home. It's closer."

"We'd have to go against the crowd," Sam said.

That seemed like an impossible task.

"We'll take the back streets," Rachel said. But even the back streets were filling up.

"I know!" Sam said suddenly. "The hospital. It's only a few blocks from here."

"Yes, and Papa might still be there."

"Even if he's not, we could use a telephone."

"All right, let's do it."

With new determination, they turned to join the still-swelling crowd.

"Sam, how many people do you think are here?"

"Must be thousands," Sam answered. "They just keep coming. The crowd goes on for blocks and blocks."

They walked a block toward the hospital. Rachel felt as though they were going only a few inches at a time. It was hard to keep the pie level. Cherry filling had started to seep through the towel wrapped around the pie tin. It stuck to Rachel's hand and dampened her sapphire cloak, turning it a deep purple that reminded her of blood. She shivered.

They came to a standstill, pressed in on every side.

"What's happening, Sam?" Rachel shouted. She could hardly breathe. "I can't see."

A tall man next to her leaned toward Rachel. "I'll tell you what's happening. We're going to teach that Thomas Lowry a lesson once and for all. You can be proud to be here today. This will be a day Minneapolis will not soon forget."

Rachel did not answer the man. Without looking up at him, she moved even closer to Sam.

Sam was craning his neck, trying to see through the crowd.

"I think there's a streetcar up there," he said. "I saw it a minute ago, but I can't see it anymore."

Rachel was too short to see anything. A jolt from behind pushed her into the woman in front of her. The pie oozed some more.

"Wait!" Sam cried. "The streetcar is still there. It's just covered with people."

"People are riding the streetcar?"

"No, they're climbing all over it."

"Climbing?"

"Yes, standing on top of it, hanging out the windows."

Rachel's stomach was flipping. "Sam, I'm scared."

Then she remembered the streetcar they had seen earlier. "Sam! Is it the same streetcar we saw earlier?"

"Probably. There haven't been any others going by."

"Annalina's father! What if that was Annalina's father driving the streetcar?"

Sam was silent.

"Sam, we have to find out!"

"I never said I was sure it was him. It just looked like him. It could have been another Swedish immigrant."

"Or it could have been Mr. Borg."

"We don't know that for sure."

"You're the one who thought it was him!"

"I was probably wrong," Sam insisted. He pushed Rachel in front of him and pointed through an opening in the crowd. "Look, see for yourself what is happening."

The crowd had parted just enough for Rachel to spot the streetcar. Men, women, and children of all ages were scrambling up the sides of the car and hoisting themselves to the top. Those on top offered their hands to pull more people to the top of the car. Rachel could not imagine how there was room for one more person up there. Still they climbed.

"I don't see any horses to pull the car," Rachel observed.

Sam stood on his tiptoes and craned his neck. "I don't either. They must have unhitched them."

A man with a bullhorn leaned out the side of the car.

"Thomas Lowry, if you are out there," he shouted, "take note. You cannot ignore us. You cannot simply hire more drivers. What will happen when you have no more streetcars?"

"What does he mean, Sam?" Rachel asked.

"Rachel, I think we have to get out of here. Now!" Sam pulled Rachel forcefully along. She stumbled as she tried to keep her balance. "We have to get to the hospital."

But to get to the hospital, they had to pass the streetcar. Sam wound his way steadily through the crowd.

"People are getting out now," Rachel said as they got closer to the streetcar.

"Don't pay any attention," Sam said. "Concentrate on the hospital."

"But why are they getting out? Are they finished?"

"How would I know?" Sam snapped. "I just want to get out of here."

"But, Sam—"

Sam spun around. His mouth opened to speak, but then he saw what Rachel was looking at. A row of men had lined themselves up along one side of the streetcar. Bracing their feet solidly, they leaned into the car. It rocked from side to side. Whooping, more men joined the effort. Dozens were pushing on the side of the street-car. The car rocked some more. They pushed again. Now the car was tipping.

Sam jerked Rachel back. The car tumbled over on one side. With a mighty groan, the joints on one end gave way, and the top of the car splintered off. A wheel broke loose and skidded through the crowd. Once again, the mob scrambled to stand on top of the wreckage. In only a few seconds, it was impossible to see what they were standing on. A mountain of people had arisen in the middle of Minneapolis. The horses had been unhitched. Now they thundered down the street, whinnying and thrashing their hooves. The crowd parted to let them pass. No one tried to catch the frightened animals.

"You are destroying private property!" The shout came from the middle of the street. Four men, their fists raised in the air, charged toward the buried streetcar.

The man with the bullhorn laughed. "If you are Mr. Lowry's men, you are too late."

"Have you no respect for something that doesn't belong to you?"

"Just like Mr. Lowry respects us, eh? He thinks he owns us. Well, he doesn't. He won't even come to the arbitration table. When will he show us the respect we deserve?"

Lowry's men hurled themselves toward the man with the bull-horn. He toppled over backward. Rachel could hear fists smacking flesh. Blood spattered faces and clothing. The mob on the top of the streetcar moved like an avalanche down to the street. It was too late for words. Fists were swinging in every direction.

"Rachel, we have to get out of here now!" Sam shouted. He took firm hold of her arm and pulled her along.

Suddenly a man in a brown coat fell backward right into Sam.

Sam lost his balance—and his grip on Rachel—and was swallowed up into the mob. His sack of potatoes hit the ground and split open. Seizing the opportunity, some teenagers scrambled to pick up the potatoes and began heaving them into the crowd.

Still clutching her crumbling pie, Rachel searched for Sam. Everything was happening so fast! The crowd swirled around her. Rachel was getting dizzy. She was afraid she would fall down, too.

"Sam!"

"Rachel!" came the muffled response.

"Sam, where are you?"

Then she spotted his boots. Sam was sprawled across the middle of the street. In their rush to join the fracas, people were stepping on him or stepping over him. No one stopped to help him. Rachel forced her way into the flow of traffic and jerked to a stop in front of Sam. A woman hurtling past knocked the pie out of Rachel's arms. The pie landed upside down. Cherries oozed through the towel. Then someone stepped on the pie tin, smashing it beyond repair.

"My pie!" Rachel moaned.

Sam was on his feet. "Forget the pie."

"Sam, are you all right?" Rachel examined her brother. She saw footmarks on his jacket, and his face was bruised. Blood trickled from a cut on his left cheek.

"I don't think it's anything serious," Sam said, "but I'm glad we're headed to the hospital."

"I wish Mama was here," Rachel moaned.

"I just hope Mama and Carrie are all right."

With their elbows linked, they started off again. Inch by inch, they edged their way to the outskirts of the crowd. Finally the hospital was in sight. But Rachel knew it would take them a long time to go even a few blocks.

Whoever had been driving the streetcar had long ago abandoned it. Rachel found herself scanning the faces in the crowd, looking to see if Mr. Borg was there.

Tripping and jostling their way through the crowd, Sam and Rachel made slow but steady progress. When they reached the hospital door, Sam pushed it open and they tumbled in.

CHAPTER 10
At the Hospital

Inside the main hospital door, Sam and Rachel stopped for a moment to catch their breath. They dropped into a pair of empty wooden chairs away from the door.

"Are you all right, Sam?" Rachel asked. "You look pale."

Sam raised one hand to the side of his head. "I have an awful headache. I think I got kicked."

"I couldn't even see what happened to you," Rachel said.

"I got knocked over, that's all. I should have been paying better attention to what was happening."

"Don't be silly," Rachel said. "You couldn't help what happened."

Sam leaned his head back against the wall behind him and closed his eyes.

"Maybe you need a doctor," Rachel said. "The cut on your cheek is still bleeding." She reached into the pocket of her pastel plaid skirt for a handkerchief and dabbed at the cut.

"I'll be all right," Sam responded, wincing a little bit. "But we should try to find out if Papa is still here."

Rachel surveyed the lobby. It was crowded. Sam and Rachel were not the only ones who had come to the hospital to escape the chaos of the streets. They had gotten the last two empty chairs.

"You stay here," Rachel said, "and I'll try to find out if Papa is still here."

Across the congested room was a large wooden desk painted

green, and behind the desk was a flustered nurse. Nearly two dozen people swarmed around her trying to ask their questions. Some of them were scraped and bruised and probably wanted a doctor. Others were just asking a lot of questions. The nurse kept looking down the hall as if she wanted to escape.

Rachel went and stood at the desk. She knew that the nurse at that desk would have a big black book that would show whether her father had signed out and left the hospital. Ordinarily it was a simple thing to approach the desk and ask about Papa. But Rachel could not get anywhere near the desk that day. The nurse would not pay attention to a small ten-year-old when twenty adults were pressing in on her. Rachel tried to figure out if there was a line so she could get in it. Three times she was pushed away by someone much bigger than she.

Finally she turned back to Sam. He had not moved the whole time she was gone.

"The nurse is too busy," Rachel reported. "I think I'll go up to the ward on the third floor. That's where Papa usually sees his patients. You can stay here."

"No," Sam said, "we should stay together."

Inwardly, Rachel was relieved Sam wanted to stay with her.

Sam pulled himself to his feet, and they started down the hall to find the dark stairs that would take them to the third floor. At the top of the stairs they turned left and continued on to the ward. Sam cautiously pushed open the door to the large room. Sixteen beds were arranged in neat rows down both sides of the ward. Several nurses made their way swiftly from one bed to the next to make sure the patients were comfortable.

"I don't see Papa."

"I don't, either," Sam said. "Where else should we look?"

"We can check the other wards," Rachel suggested.

"You'll do no such thing!" barked a voice behind them.

Sam and Rachel spun around to find the ward's head nurse scowling down at them. "This is a hospital, not a playground," she said.

"We're looking for Dr. Borland," Sam said. "He's our father."

"I'm aware of that, but children do not belong in a hospital ward."

"We have to find him," Rachel said.

"There!" The nurse pointed to a small, dark room across the hall. "You may wait there. When I see Dr. Borland, I will tell him where to find you."

"My brother is hurt," Rachel said. "He needs to see a doctor."

The nurse narrowed her eyes and studied Sam's face. In the same harsh tone, she said, "That's a nasty cut. I'll send in a cold pack. But you must wait in there!" She pointed emphatically to the small room. Sam and Rachel shuffled across the hall reluctantly.

The room was furnished with four wooden chairs and a small table. A round window high in the wall provided the only light.

"Do you think she will really tell Papa we're here?"

"I hope so," Sam answered. "And I hope she sends that cold pack."

"Does your head hurt very much?" Rachel asked softly.

Sam nodded.

They waited in that room for what seemed like hours. Sam laid his head down on the table. Rachel went to the doorway and looked out. The third floor seemed much busier than it usually was. Nurses moved down the hall with quick, purposeful steps. Their crisp uniforms swished and rustled with every step. Doctors in white jackets hung their stethoscopes around their necks and looked worried.

Suddenly Rachel jumped out into the hall.

"Papa!"

"Rachel! What are you doing here?"

Rachel took her father's hand and pulled him into the small room. "Sam! Are you all right?" Papa put his hand on Sam's flushed cheek.

"He got kicked in the head," Rachel explained.

Then she told Papa the whole story of how the family had started out for the Stockards' for Easter dinner, and Mama and Carrie had disappeared.

Papa made Sam sit up so he could look in his eyes. "I don't see any sign of serious injury."

"I just have a headache," Sam said. "I'll be all right. But what about Mama and Carrie?"

"There's a telephone down at the end of the hall," Papa said. "We'll go call the Stockards and see if Mama and Carrie made it over there."

But Mama and Carrie were not at the Stockards'. No one but the Stockard family was there. Aunt Linda had heard about the tipped-over streetcar and the riot. In fact, she told Papa that two streetcars had been tipped over, not just one. But she had not heard from Mama.

"That means they are still out there somewhere," Rachel said.

"They could have gone in another building," Sam said.

Papa looked worried—very worried. "I want to look for them."

"But Papa, the riot!" Rachel protested.

"I'll settle the two of you in a safe, quiet place. Sam, maybe we can find you a bed to rest on until your head stops hurting. Then I'm going to go out to look for your mother and sister."

"Dr. Borland, come quick!" It was the head nurse. "They need you down on the first floor."

"What happened?"

"Several more men have just come in, and they are hurt quite badly."

Papa sighed. "All right, I'll be right there."

"Papa, don't leave us here," Rachel pleaded.

"Come with me," Papa responded, "but stay out of the way. I don't want you to get hurt."

Papa thundered down the stairs. Rachel and Sam did their best to keep up with him. Sam groaned with every step. The lobby was even more crowded than it had been earlier. Papa made his way to a corner of the room and ducked through a door into a room behind the main lobby.

Rachel gasped when she saw the first patient. "It's the man with the bullhorn!" she said to Sam.

"I don't think he thought anyone could hurt him," Sam said.

The man's left arm did not look right. The skin was scraped off one side of his face, and his right eye was bruised and swollen.

"What do you think happened to him?" Rachel asked.

"It was probably those management men," Sam answered. "Remember? The three men who ran up right after the streetcar fell over?"

Rachel nodded. "But there were only three of them—three against the whole crowd."

"They must have had other friends with them. Besides, with a baseball bat or a heavy stick, all it would take is a couple of swings."

Careful to stay out of the way, they watched their father at work. He set the broken arm and gave the nurses instructions about the other injuries.

"When can I get out of here, Doc?" the man asked.

"I'd like you to stay a couple days," Papa told the man.

"I can't do that. I have no money to pay you. I'm a streetcar driver."

"We'll worry about that later," Papa said. "I think you have two broken ribs. You must be taken care of." He turned to the nurse. "Make sure he gets a bed in one of the wards."

"Here comes the next one," the nurse responded, as an orderly wheeled in another patient.

"I know this man," Papa said.

Rachel's heart leaped. Mr. Borg? She lurched forward for a better look. No, it was not Mr. Borg.

"I've treated him before," Papa continued. "He's one of Thomas Lowry's managers."

"Then he's a dog!" growled the first patient.

"Orderly," Papa said, nodding his head at his first patient. "I think you can take him upstairs now."

"Dog, he's a dog!" shouted the man as the orderly wheeled him away.

Papa turned his attention to his new patient, who was unconscious. With a thumb, Papa pushed one of the man's eyelids open. "I don't like the way his pupils look," he told the nurse.

The nurse from the front desk stuck her head in the room.

"Doctor, there are two more coming in now."

"Aren't there any other doctors around?" Papa asked.

"Dr. James is upstairs with a critical patient. Dr. Michaels is delivering a baby."

"Is there no one else?"

"It's Easter Sunday, Doctor," the nurse responded. "Most of the doctors did their rounds hours ago and went home to Easter dinner."

"We need help," Papa insisted. "Get on the telephone and call Dr. Lee and Dr. Sheridan. Now!"

"Yes, Doctor."

The man on the gurney in front of Papa began gasping for air. Papa held the man's mouth open and pushed down on his tongue with a flat wooden stick.

"His airway is blocked! We'll have to intubate!"

Nurse Howard flew into action and produced a narrow tube.

"Hold his mouth open," Papa ordered as he started forcing the tube down the man's mouth. The patient thrashed. Two more nurses came in to help hold him down. In another moment, Papa had the tube down the man's throat, and he was breathing steadily.

Rachel could hardly bear to watch. She scrunched up against the wall as tightly as she could. Sam had found a spot in the corner where he could sit down and lean his head against the wall.

Papa stepped back from his patient just as the orderlies brought in two more men.

"What do we have?" Papa asked.

The nurses gave the best report they could on the injuries they had observed. Blood and broken bones filled the small room.

Sam and Rachel pressed themselves up against the wall, hardly able to take in what they were seeing.

"Doctor, perhaps your children would be more comfortable somewhere else," Nurse Howard suggested.

"No, they're fine," Papa said without looking up.

"It's okay, Papa," Rachel said. "We can go wait in the lobby."

Papa glanced up for just a second. "Don't go anywhere else, do you understand? And if any fighting breaks out, you come right back in here."

"Yes, Papa."

"Miss Howard, please make sure that my son has a place to sit down."

"Yes, Doctor."

Nurse Howard ushered Sam and Rachel back out to the main lobby.

When they were alone in the crowded lobby, Sam said quietly, "They are all the same."

Rachel turned to him, puzzled.

"When they are hurt," Sam said, "they are all the same. They need a doctor. They all have the same broken bones and bloody faces. And Papa helps them all. He doesn't care if they are union or management."

Rachel scanned the lobby. Sam was right. Everyone was the same.

She could not tell just by looking whether the woman in the green coat was waiting for a union husband or a management husband. She could not tell if the children playing in the corner belonged to a union father or a management father.

She found herself looking for Mr. Borg once again and praying that he was safe.

CHAPTER 11
Where's Mama?

In the lobby, Rachel picked up a newspaper someone had abandoned. The headlines for Easter Sunday 1889 cried out: "STRIKE CONTINUES. LOWRY SAYS NO NEGOTIATIONS." "RESTLESS DRIVERS THREATEN ACTION." "UNION DEMANDS HEIGHTEN."

Rachel scanned the beginning of one article: "Thomas Lowry, owner of the Minneapolis Streetcar Company, insists that he will not submit to arbitration to settle the streetcar strike. 'In the future,' said Lowry, 'the Minneapolis Street Railway will run its own business instead of having it run by a union.' Although the business has suffered greatly during the strike, Lowry continues to hire replacement drivers. He has brought in a hundred men from Kansas City to drive the routes abandoned by union drivers. If Lowry continues to refuse arbitration, drivers are threatening further action to force his cooperation."

Rachel tossed the paper aside. The news was already old. The drivers were no longer threatening action. They had taken action that morning. Their action had brought Rachel and Sam to the hospital lobby instead of to the Stockards' house for a scrumptious Easter dinner. Rachel's stomach was starting to growl. She thought about the cherry pie, and her eyes filled with tears.

Where had Sam gone? Rachel glanced around the lobby, searching for her brother. They had promised Papa not to wander off. Her eyes darted from person to person until at last she found him.

Sam had shuffled up to the big green desk. The lobby was just as full as it had been before, but the crowd seemed more organized. A different nurse was on duty. She seemed less flustered and more in control. "The line forms to the left," the nurse called out every few minutes. She answered questions and passed out forms for people to fill out. Every once in a while, someone wanted to ask a question without waiting in line. But the nurse firmly said, "The line forms to the left."

Papa had been out to the lobby to check on Sam and Rachel two times in the last two hours. No new emergencies had come in for more than an hour, and Dr. Lee and Dr. Sheridan had finally showed up to help Papa. Rachel thought that things ought to be settling down. She wondered where Papa was now. She supposed he was at the bedside of the patient he had intubated.

She knew Papa had read a lot of articles about intubation before he ever tried it. But finally he was convinced that the only way to help some patients breathe was to intubate—to put a long tube down their throats so they could get air to their lungs. Then Papa would make sure the patient was all right and breathing on his own before he would relax.

Papa was a good doctor. Rachel was sure of that. But she wanted to know how much longer the good doctor would have to stay at the hospital.

Rachel eyed the long line ahead of Sam at the green reception desk. She did not want to stand in that line with him just to ask if the nurse knew what her father was doing. How could that nurse know? She had been in the lobby the whole time. Rachel got to her feet and moved toward the door that led to the examination room behind the lobby. Maybe Papa was still there.

As she got closer to the room, Rachel cocked her ear. She did not hear any noises coming from the room. *Probably all the patients have been moved to the wards,* she thought. But she wanted to check the room just to be sure Papa was not there. With her hand on the door-knob, she turned to look around. She did not see Nurse Howard any-where. Still with her back to the door, she turned the knob and leaned back on the door and pushed it open.

The clatter that followed told Rachel that the room had not been empty. When she got the door open, she saw a dismayed Nurse Howard scrambling to pick up a tray. Medical instruments had scattered all over the floor.

The nurse scowled at Rachel. "Look what you did!"

"I'm sorry," Rachel exclaimed. "I'll help you pick everything up." She stooped to the floor and retrieved a pair of steel tongs.

"Don't touch anything," Miss Howard said. "Some of these are delicate instruments. Now they'll have to be cleaned all over again."

"I–I'm sorry," Rachel muttered.

"Perhaps you haven't noticed that we are rather busy around here today."

"Of–of course," Rachel stammered. "I was just looking for my father."

"As you can see, he's not here. Now scat."

Rachel scurried out of the room and back to the lobby. Sam had taken a seat again, and Rachel sank into the chair beside him, her heart pounding.

Sam chuckled. "Something tells me you've been doing something you shouldn't have been doing."

Rachel was not amused. "I was just looking for Papa."

"He said to wait here. The nurse said he's busy setting a broken leg."

"He told us to wait a long time ago. Why isn't he finished?"

"A lot of people were hurt in the riot," Sam said. "Papa is a doctor. He has to take care of them."

"But what about Mama and Carrie?" Rachel asked. "Papa was going to look for them."

"They haven't shown up here," Sam said. "That probably means they are all right."

"How can you be so sure?"

"I'm not sure. But it makes sense."

"I'm getting hungry," Rachel said. "We were supposed to eat hours ago. I didn't eat any breakfast because I wanted to be sure I had room for pie."

"I'm sorry about your pie," Sam said softly.

"Right now I would settle for burned toast."

"Me, too."

Rachel stood up again.

"Sit down, Rachel," Sam said. "Just relax. There's nothing you can do but wait."

"I can't. I'm tired of sitting. I'm tired of this room. I'm tired of this day!"

"It has been a long day," Sam agreed.

Rachel started pacing. The crowd in the lobby was thinning out. People with minor injuries were being released, and their families took them home. Rachel stood and looked out the window on the side of the building. *The street looks better,* she thought. Not so many people were roaming around. As the afternoon gave way to evening, people took shelter in their homes.

Suddenly Rachel lurched forward. She had been pushed from behind. Remembering the feeling of being pushed in the middle of the mob earlier in the day, she panicked for a second. Then she spun around. As she did, Carrie grabbed her around the waist.

"Carrie! You're all right!" Rachel exclaimed. "Where's Mama?"

"Right here," came Mama's voice.

Rachel threw herself into her mother's embrace. Sam joined the reunion.

"I'll go find Papa," he offered. Off he went, before Rachel could tell him not to bother looking in the examination room behind the lobby.

In almost no time, Sam was back with Papa. Rachel smiled, relieved, as her parents embraced, and then Papa gave Carrie a messy kiss on the forehead.

"Over here," Papa said, and he herded his family to an empty corner of the lobby. "I'm so glad you're all right. But where have you been?"

"I didn't know what to think when I lost track of Sam and Rachel," Mama said. "I had to trust that the Lord would take care of them. It was all I could do to keep track of Carrie in that mob."

"Papa, there were millions and millions of people," Carrie said.

Mama smiled. "Thousands at least. I've never seen such a mob, even on a parade day."

"So where did you go?" Rachel wanted to know.

"We stayed to the edge of the crowd as much as we could," Mama answered. "I tried to look for you at the next corner from where I lost you. But there were too many people! And they were doing crazy things!"

"We went shopping," Carrie blurted out.

"Shopping?" Rachel was confused.

"Not exactly," Mama said, "but we saw Mr. Johanssen in the crowd, and he opened up his shop for us. He kept going on to find any women and children who needed help."

"That's a relief," Papa said. "Remind me never to charge him for medical care again!"

"We saw women and children in the street," Sam said. "But some of them were helping with the riot."

"I know," Mama said sadly. "Some of the children didn't understand what was going on. They either got scared, or they got excited and joined in."

"Mama," Rachel said, "I never found Mr. Borg. If all the trouble is over, maybe I could go see if he's all right."

"Rachel, you are sweet and thoughtful to want to do that," Mama said, "but we can't be sure the streets are safe yet."

"Sam could go with me."

Mama shook her head. "We'll have to find out about Mr. Borg another way."

"This is the nearest hospital," Sam said. "If he didn't come here, he's probably not hurt."

"He wouldn't come here," Rachel said, "because he doesn't have any money to pay doctors."

"If he were seriously hurt," Papa said, "someone would have brought him here anyway."

"I'm hungry," Carrie complained. "When are we going to have Easter dinner?"

Mama and Papa looked at each other.

"It looks like we'll have to skip Easter dinner with the family this year," Mama said. "But we can have a simple meal with our own family."

"What will we eat?"

"Let's see what we have."

"I dropped the cherry pie," Rachel said sadly. "I hung on to it as long as I could."

"I'm sure you did," Mama said.

"And they were throwing the potatoes in the crowd," Sam said.

"That's all right," Mama answered. "The potatoes were not cooked anyway."

"Then what do we have?" Rachel asked.

"I have biscuits!" Carrie proclaimed. "They're a little squashed, but I still have them."

"And I've got corn pudding," Mama said, "and apple pie. I'm sorry it's not the pie you made, Rachel, but it is a pie."

"Can we eat now?" Carrie said. "I'm too hungry to wait until we get home."

Mama and Papa looked at each other again. It was well past suppertime. No one had eaten since before church that morning.

"Certainly," Papa said. "I'm sure I can find some of the trays they use to feed the patients."

While Papa went to find the trays, Mama pulled a little table out of the corner of the room and set the food on it. The bread really was squashed. Rachel figured Carrie must have been holding it tightly when she was frightened. Rachel did not blame her little sister for squashing the bread.

When Papa returned, they gathered around the little table on their knees.

"It's not much of an Easter dinner," Papa said, "but we have a lot to give thanks for."

They held hands as Papa prayed. "Lord, we are grateful that You have protected our family during the danger today. Thank You for bringing us safely back together. And on this Easter Sunday, we give thanks for the power of the resurrection, when Jesus Christ was raised from the dead so that we could have peace with God. May You grant peace to our city tonight. Amen."

Mama started tearing the bread into chunks. Papa had brought forks for the corn pudding and apple pie.

"Dr. Borland," called the nurse from the desk, "they need you in the back again."

Papa sighed. "Go ahead and eat. I'll be back as soon as I can."

Rachel watched reluctantly as Papa disappeared once again.

CHAPTER 12

A Birthday and a Baseball Plan

A few days after the riot, Rachel and her mother were working about the house. Sam had left for baseball practice, and Carrie was with friends. As usual, Papa was not expected home from work until late.

"Rachel, don't you have a birthday coming up?" Mama said, brushing a stray strand of hair out of her eyes. "How would you like to celebrate this year?"

Rachel put the towel that she was folding onto the pile of freshly laundered linens. "You know, I think I would like to have just a small party with a few friends."

Rachel had been giving her birthday some thought. She was finding it harder and harder to be in the middle of the conflict between Colleen and Janie. They were her oldest friends. She could barely remember a time when they hadn't played together. Now she was torn between the two—and she didn't like the feeling.

And then there was Annalina. Rachel enjoyed being with her and teaching her English. If only she could bring Annalina and Colleen and Janie together! Rachel felt frustrated that the other girls in her class still did not want to be friends with Annalina. If they just got to know her, Rachel was sure they would like her as much as she did. But how could she help the other girls understand Annalina?

Maybe she could start with Colleen and Janie.

"Who would you like to invite?" Mama seemed relieved that Rachel wasn't asking for a big party.

"Just Annalina—and Colleen and Janie. I'll invite them tomorrow. Could we have a cake and some ice cream?"

Mama smiled. "Sure."

As she went back to folding her laundry, Rachel could not help but worry a bit about her plan to bring her friends together.

The next baseball practice, on the Saturday after the riot, Rachel tagged along with Sam. She loved watching baseball, even practice baseball, and the boys never seemed to mind if she was there. She settled on one of the wooden benches at the edge of the field and leaned forward, anxious to see how things would go today.

The practice did not start out very well. The players straggled to the field late; some of them never arrived at all. Simon came, but no matter how many questions the others asked, he would not explain why he had not played in the game against the Seventh Street Spades.

Rachel knew that her brother had an idea for making his team better. They needed a coach. All the "real" teams had a coach. Sam and Rachel had talked it over, and they knew just who would be the perfect guy for the job—their cousin Seth.

"We've been playing together since we were nine," Rachel heard Sam tell his teammates, "and we do pretty well."

"That's right!" exclaimed Steve. "We're the best."

"The best," echoed Elwood.

"But I think we could be better, don't you?" Sam challenged his team.

Heads started bobbing.

"I know just what we need," Sam said. "We need someone with experience to work with us, to teach us, to help us figure out some good plays."

"Are you talking about a coach?" Joe asked.

"That's right," Sam answered. "We could get our own coach. Some of the other teams are starting to do that."

"I heard that the Oak Lake team has a coach," Elwood said.

"Why can't we have a coach, too?" Sam asked. "What do you think, Joe?"

Joe shrugged. "We're doing all right on our own, but we could probably do better with a coach."

"That's exactly what I was thinking," Sam said.

Simon was starting to warm up to the idea. "We could find someone older than we are—but not too old."

"It has to be someone who really loves baseball," Steve said. "When you're trying to win a game, attitude counts more than anything else. You can have all the skill in the world, but if your attitude is not right, you'll get nowhere."

"Do you really think a coach could help us?" Jim asked.

"Sure!" Sam responded. "We'll find someone who knows how to throw pitches that are hard to hit, someone who can help us with our swings."

"Someone who can hit long fly balls for us to practice catching," Steve added.

"Exactly!"

"But where would we find someone like that?" Simon asked. "Who is going to have time to help a boys' team?"

"I think I know someone who would do it," Sam said. He held his breath, getting ready to speak the name he had in mind.

"Who?" Simon asked.

"Yeah, who?" Jim wondered.

"Seth Stockard."

"Who's Seth Stockard?" Elwood asked.

"I know who that is," interrupted Simon. "That's your cousin."

"He's my second cousin, actually," Sam clarified. "He loves baseball, and he's really good at it."

"Has he ever been a baseball coach before?" Steve asked. "We need someone with experience, lots of it."

"I don't think he's ever been a coach," Sam said, "but he goes to professional games all the time. He understands the strategies they use. He could teach them to us."

"And you really think he would do it?" Jim was still skeptical.

"I think all we have to do is ask him."

"Wait a minute," Simon said. "How old is Seth Stockard?"

"He's eighteen."

"Does he go to college?"

"He's going to go in the fall," Sam said. "He's going to be a scientist."

Simon still looked doubtful. "What does he do now?"

Sam took a deep breath and gave the answer he had hoped to avoid. "He has a temporary job at the railroad station."

"So he's a union man," Simon said flatly.

Sam remembered the day he had seen Seth passing out union leaflets. "The important thing is that Seth understands baseball," Sam insisted.

"Attitude is everything," Steve said. "We don't need someone coming in here and spreading union propaganda."

"Who said anything about the unions?" Sam countered. "We're talking about a baseball coach. Seth would be perfect."

"Well. . ." Simon leaned on a bat. "You did say his job at the railroad was just temporary. He probably hasn't joined the union himself."

"So what if he has joined the union?" Jim snapped.

"We have to be careful who we have around here," Simon said.

"What is that supposed to mean?" Jim pressed.

"Yeah, what is that supposed to mean?" Tad echoed.

Rachel thought Tad seemed eager for Simon and Jim to go nose to nose.

"Take it easy," Sam said. "We're talking about baseball, remember?"

"Doesn't Seth's father work at a bank?" Simon asked.

"Yes, that's right."

"So he doesn't come from a union family."

"That's not what matters. We need a coach, and he can help us."

Elwood was watching Steve carefully. Joe shuffled around the edge of the circle acting like he was not interested in the discussion. Rachel could see that Tad's eyes were bright with the hope of an argument. Hank was so nervous his chin twitched.

"I say we give it a try," Steve said finally.

"Me, too," Elwood immediately added.

"I don't suppose it could hurt," Jim conceded.

Rachel was watching Simon. His jaw worked back and forth while he thought about the question. Rachel clasped her hands nervously in her lap, hoping that Sam's plan would succeed.

"All right, we'll give it a try," Simon finally said. "But the minute there is any talk about union nonsense, he leaves the team. Agreed?"

"Agreed." Sam nodded.

Rachel sighed and sat back on the bench. It was a fair compromise.

CHAPTER 13

A Special Supper

"I hope Annalina likes chicken," Rachel said, as she turned over a drumstick in the simmering lard.

"I'm sure she will like anything you cook." Mama glanced over Rachel's shoulder at the frying chicken.

"I tried to ask her what she likes," Rachel continued, "but she didn't understand. The other girls were laughing at me when I was squawking like a chicken."

Mama chuckled. "It probably was funny."

"Annalina still did not understand. So I don't know if she eats chicken. I don't know anything about what Swedish people eat."

"What does she bring for her lunch at school?" Mama whacked the ends off a bunch of carrots.

"She usually just brings bread. Sometimes she has a piece of fruit."

"Then I'm sure she'll enjoy your biscuits and apple pie."

The biscuits were already out of the oven and wrapped in a cloth to keep them warm until dinner.

"Annalina's mother makes the most beautiful bread. It's not just a loaf or biscuits. She twists the dough into braids, and the crusts look shiny."

"She probably brushes the top with an egg mixture," Mama said.

"I want her to teach me how to make Swedish bread."

"Why don't you ask her?"

"I will—as soon as I learn enough Swedish or Annalina learns enough English to translate."

"That won't be long," Mama said, "considering how much time you spend with her working on English."

"I'll be so glad when she learns enough English to really talk. On the day after the riot, I tried to ask her if her father was all right. But she didn't understand. It was so frustrating!"

"I'm sure it was frustrating for Annalina, too," Mama said. "But at least you found out that it was not Mr. Borg driving that streetcar on Sunday."

"I was so relieved. He was home safe. It was someone who looked like him."

Mama glanced at the perfectly formed pie on the counter next to her daughter. Rachel followed her mother's eye.

"Is it time to put the pie in the oven?" Rachel turned over another piece of chicken. The hot lard sizzled and splattered.

"Yes, put the pie in," Mama said. "That way it will be fresh and warm at just the right time."

Rachel opened the oven, which was still warm from the biscuits, and set the apple pie in the middle.

"Don't forget to watch the time." Mama tossed the carrots she had chopped into a pot of boiling water. "Linda and Agnes were disappointed that they didn't get to taste your pie on Easter."

"Me, too! It was my first pie, and it was perfect, but no one got to take even a bite."

"I'm sure this one will not go to waste."

"Mama, are we going to have another family dinner?" Rachel asked. "Can we make up for missing Easter dinner?"

"Agnes has suggested that. We all want to do it."

"Even Uncle Ernest and Uncle Stanley?"

Mama sighed. "Ernest and Stanley have finally found something to agree on. They have different opinions about the strike, but they both think that turning over a streetcar and starting a riot was not necessary."

"Does that mean they're ready to be friends again?"

"It might be a first step."

Someone knocked on the front door. "Annalina!" Rachel snatched up a towel and tried to rub the grease off her hands.

By the time Rachel got to the front door, Carrie already had it open. Annalina looked relieved to see Rachel.

"This is my sister, Carrie." Rachel took Annalina's hand and pulled her into the living room. Annalina smiled nervously.

"And this is my mother," Rachel continued.

Annalina nodded her head politely. With one hand, she clutched a small bundle close to her chest.

"Carrie," Mama said, "run and find Papa and Sam. Tell them our guest is here."

"Come in and sit down." Rachel led Annalina to a chair. "Sit." She demonstrated by sitting in the chair next to Annalina. The Swedish girl sat down, still clutching her bundle. Her faded yellow calico dress hung down over her scuffed brown boots. But her eyes were bright with anticipation.

"I'm going to check on the chicken," Mama said.

Rachel was tempted to flap her elbows and squawk but decided against it. It was too late to change the menu. Either Annalina would eat chicken or she would not.

Carrie returned with Papa and Sam. Annalina smiled at Sam, whom she recognized.

"This is my papa," Rachel said.

Papa extended his hand. "I am pleased to meet you."

Annalina put her small white hand in Papa's big hand. "Nice." Now she thrust the small bundle toward Rachel.

"What is this?" Rachel asked.

"Give," Annalina said.

"Give? Is it a gift?"

Annalina nodded. "I give."

Rachel laid the bundle in her lap and began unwrapping it. Annalina's family was very poor. What kind of gift could she have brought? Rachel gasped in delight when the package lay open in her lap.

"Dolls!" Carrie squealed.

Three small painted wooden dolls lay in Rachel's lap. They were only a few inches tall, but they were painted with exquisite detail in bright colors and a glossy finish.

"These are beautiful!" Rachel exclaimed. "Look, Mama." She held up the dolls as her mother came back into the room. "Look what Annalina brought."

Mama picked up one of the dolls. "Look at that little face! Why, Rachel, it almost looks like you."

Rachel turned to her friend. "Annalina, where did you get these?"

Annalina did not understand.

"Buy?" Rachel said. "Store?"

Annalina shook her head. "No. No store. I make."

"You made these?" Somehow the dolls seemed even more beautiful now.

Annalina gestured as if she were holding a carving knife. "Papa."

"Your papa carves the dolls?"

Now Annalina moved her fingers delicately as if she were painting. "Annalina."

"Your papa carves the dolls, and you paint them?"

Annalina nodded vigorously.

"They are a beautiful gift," Rachel said. "Thank you."

"I think supper is just about ready," Mama said.

"Great!" Sam said. "I'm famished."

Rachel showed Annalina the way to the kitchen. When they had all sat down around the table, Annalina bowed her head along with all the Borlands, and Papa gave thanks for the food and for Rachel's new friend. Mama had put the chicken on a platter, and she started passing it around the table. The boiled carrots followed, along with a bowl of mashed potatoes.

"Where are the biscuits?" Carrie asked.

"We almost forgot." Rachel popped over to the sideboard and fetched the basket of biscuits.

Carrie took two biscuits and passed the basket to Sam.

Rachel watched Annalina carefully as she took a small portion of everything that was passed. When the platter of chicken came to Annalina, she started giggling.

"What's so funny?" Rachel asked.

Annalina covered her mouth in embarrassment. But she could not stop giggling. Then she flapped her elbows in the air and squawked.

The whole Borland family burst out laughing.

"Yes," Rachel said, flapping her elbows, too. "Chicken."

"I think she understands now." Mama smiled.

"Chicken," repeated Rachel.

"Shikeen," said Annalina.

"Chicken. Do you like chicken?" Rachel asked.

Annalina picked up the chicken leg on her plate and took a big bite. Rachel leaned back in her chair, relieved.

"The chicken is delicious," Papa said. He helped himself to a second piece.

"Thank you." Rachel glanced at Annalina, and they almost started giggling again.

After a while, Mama said, "Don't forget to check the pie."

Rachel scooted her chair back and crossed the kitchen to the oven.

Peeking in, she said, "I think it's done." Protecting her hands with two folded dishtowels, she removed the pie from the hot oven and set it on the sideboard.

"It looks perfect!" The crust had baked to a golden brown. Steam rose through the holes Rachel had pricked in the top of the pie.

Carrie pushed her plate away. "I'm ready for pie."

Mama inspected Carrie's plate to see that she had eaten all of her supper. "All right," Mama said, "but don't take more pie than you can eat."

Rachel took a stack of plates down from a shelf and started serving the pie. Mama cleared the dinner plates from the table.

Rachel set a slice of pie in front of her little sister and another in front of her brother. "You two have the privilege of being the first tasters."

Carrie stuck her fork in the pie and shoveled a piece into her mouth. Sam did the same.

As Rachel brought plates to the table for Annalina and her father, she saw Carrie spitting out her first bite of pie.

"Carrie!" Mama scolded.

"I'm sorry, Mama, but it doesn't taste like your apple pie."

"She's right." Sam's face was contorted, and his cheeks puffed out as he tried not to spit out the bite of pie. With a great effort, he forced it down his throat. "This doesn't taste like anyone's apple pie."

Rachel's heart started pounding. What was wrong with her perfect pie?

Papa gingerly took the tiniest piece of pie on the end of his fork and put it to his lips. Even before he put it in his mouth, he knew what was wrong. He started laughing.

"Rachel, how much sugar did you put in this?" Papa asked.

"One cup, just like the recipe called for."

"And where did you get the sugar from?"

Rachel whirled around to look at the canisters on the counter. Then she groaned. "I used salt!"

"A whole cup of salt!" Sam grimaced and put down his fork.

Rachel snatched away the plate she had just set in front of Annalina. Her friend was confused.

"No good," Rachel said. "No good."

"Annalina like pie," her friend said.

Rachel shook her head hard. "Not this pie. This pie is bad." She made a sour face. Rachel nudged the platter of chicken toward Annalina. "Have some more chicken."

Annalina started giggling all over again. Carrie and Sam flapped their arms. Mama and Papa roared. The kitchen full of human chickens almost made Rachel forget about her disastrous pie.

Still laughing, Mama took the plates from Sam and Carrie. "Rachel, you go visit with your friend. Papa can help me clean up tonight."

In the living room, Rachel pouted for a few minutes. She dropped her first pie in the Easter riot. Now she'd put salt in the next one. Would she ever make a pie that anyone could eat? She pushed her straggling blond hair away from her face and sighed.

Annalina's hair was neatly tied in tight braids. Rachel's hung loose round her shoulders, with two floppy bows on top of her head. She touched the end of one of Annalina's braids.

"This is pretty," she said.

Annalina reached out and took hold of Rachel's hair. With skilled fingers, she started braiding.

"Can you braid my hair?" Rachel asked.

Annalina's finger's kept moving.

"Wait," Rachel said, "I want you to do all of it." She pulled a straight-backed chair away from the wall and sat in it. Annalina combed her fingers through Rachel's hair, making it do exactly what she wanted it to do. After she had made two tight, neat braids, she moved the bows from the top of Rachel's head to the bottom of the braids. Finally, she stood back, satisfied with her work.

Rachel got up and stood in front of the brass-rimmed looking glass next to the front door. Annalina stood next to her. They smiled at their matching blond braids and blue eyes.

"You two could be sisters!" Sam had come into the room and looked at their reflection in the glass. "Rachel, you really look Swedish!"

Rachel smiled. "I think it would be fun to go to another country. Maybe someday I'll go to Sweden."

Annalina stepped away from the mirror and peered out at the darkness beyond the front door. "I go," she said quietly.

"Already?" Rachel moaned.

"Papa said he would walk Annalina home," Sam said. "She shouldn't go by herself now that it's dark."

After Papa and Annalina were gone, Mama said, "Your friend is very nice, Rachel. And you're doing a wonderful job teaching her English. She understands quite a bit."

"At least now she knows what 'chicken' means! I don't understand how anyone could not like Annalina."

CHAPTER 14

Annalina's Gift

When Rachel went to school the next morning, she still wore her hair in braids. She liked the braids, and she did not mind one bit if she looked Swedish.

"People are going to get you confused with Annalina," Sam told her.

Rachel simply tossed her braids over her shoulders and said, "I don't care."

They got to school early, twenty minutes before the bell would ring. Carrie scampered off to play with girls her own age.

"I'm going to go find some of the boys from the team and let them know Seth is coming to practice tomorrow," Sam said.

Rachel scanned the schoolyard for Annalina, but she was not there yet. Shifting her bundle of books to the other shoulder, Rachel started over to the corner of the school yard where Annalina liked to sit. She would wait for her friend there.

Instead, she nearly ran into Mariah Webster.

"Rachel Borland, what have you done to yourself?" Mariah laughed loudly.

"What do you mean?" Rachel responded, even though she knew what Mariah was talking about.

"Your hair! It's in braids!"

"So? Haven't you ever seen braids before?"

"Of course I have—just not on you."

"I never tried them before, but I like them."

"You look like you just got off the boat from Sweden."

Mariah had dark hair and dark eyes. No one would ever mistake her for a Swedish immigrant. Like Rachel's family, the Websters had been in America for generations.

"We all have to come from somewhere," Rachel said.

"Why do you want to be Swedish? What's wrong with being American?"

"What's wrong with being Swedish?" Rachel countered.

"Rachel, why are you so crazy lately? I never see you anymore. You always eat lunch with that new girl."

"Her name is Annalina. And there's plenty of room on the bench for you to sit with us."

"Now you're acting just like her, even fixing your hair the way she does. Are you going to stop speaking English?"

Rachel lifted her chin. "*Tack sa mycket.*"

"Stop it, Rachel!"

"Mariah, Swedish is just another language. Annalina is just like you and me and all the other girls. She's smart and funny and works hard. When she learns more English, you'll find out for yourself."

Mariah looked doubtful. "We've all known each other all our lives. I have enough friends already."

"But Annalina doesn't," Rachel said. "What if your father decided to move your family to Europe and you had to leave all your friends?"

Mariah was not sure what to say. "My father wouldn't do that," she muttered.

Rachel saw Annalina come through the gate. "There's Annalina now. Let's go talk to her."

"Um, you go," Mariah said. "I see Katherine coming in at the other gate, and I need to talk to her."

Mariah hurried off to Katherine and her familiar cluster of friends. Shaking her head, Rachel crossed the yard to greet Annalina. At the same moment, they put their elbows in the air and flapped and squawked.

"Chicken good," Annalina said.

"I'm glad you liked it."

Annalina smiled. "Pie not good."

"Shh. Don't tell anyone about that."

Behind them, Mariah snickered. Rachel glared at Mariah. Apparently talking to Mariah had done no good at all. Katherine, however, had stopped giggling. Rachel saw her looking at Annalina as if she was really interested in her.

They moved to a bench and put their books down. Rachel reached into the roomy pocket of her skirt and pulled out two of the dolls Annalina had given her the night before. She set them on the bench.

"These are beautiful," Rachel said. "I couldn't stand to leave them home."

Two other girls had joined Mariah and Katherine. Mariah was pointing at Rachel and Annalina.

Rachel had an idea. She held the dolls up in the air. Loudly, she said, "You did such a beautiful job painting these dolls. I hope that you will teach me how to do it." She turned the dolls in several directions. Their bright colors gleamed in the sunlight.

Annalina was puzzled.

Rachel pointed to Annalina and then herself. "You," she said slowly, "teach me." And she held her fingers together as if she were holding a paintbrush. She glanced at the other girls. They were watching.

"Painting the dolls is very difficult," Rachel said loudly. "You have a special talent. Not everyone could do such beautiful work."

Rachel knew she was talking too much—and too loudly. Annalina was not understanding. But Mariah and Katherine and the others understood. She had their attention now. In a group, they were slowly walking toward the bench where Annalina and Rachel sat. Rachel watched them out of the side of her eyes while she continued to talk to Annalina. When the four girls were close enough to cast a shadow on Annalina, Rachel turned to speak directly to them.

"Would you like to see my new dolls?" Rachel said to the girls. "Annalina gave them to me. She painted them herself."

Unsure, the other girls looked at each other. Finally Mariah nodded her head. "Okay. We'll look at them."

They gathered around the bench. Rachel passed around the two dolls.

"I've never seen anything like this," Katherine said. "Did she really paint them herself?"

"Of course she did," Rachel said. "She brought three of them to my house last night, all different sizes."

"Where does she get the dolls?"

"Her father carves them."

Mariah's eyes widened in interest. "Her father carves the dolls, and she paints them?"

Rachel nodded.

Mariah looked at Annalina, then asked Rachel, "Does she understand what we're saying?"

"Slow down, and use short words," Rachel suggested.

"Are you sure?"

"Go ahead," Rachel urged.

Mariah turned to Annalina. "Very pretty," she said, holding one of the dolls.

"Dank you." Annalina smiled.

Rachel smiled, too. The beautiful dolls were a language of their own. Girls from across the ocean could enjoy the same beauty. Annalina was going to do just fine.

As the other girls all tried to talk at once to Annalina, Rachel stood up. She was hoping to share the good news with Sam. But when she tried to catch his eye from across the school yard, she saw that things were not going as well for him this morning as they had for her. "See you in class," she told the other girls, and then she moved closer to Sam and his group of friends, hoping to hear what was going on.

"It was crazy to turn over a streetcar," Steve was saying. "The people who did that should be arrested and locked up."

"All ten thousand of them?" someone asked.

"There were ten thousand people at the riot," Steve said, "but not all of them turned over the streetcars. Only a few did that."

Rachel could still picture the faces of the men who had rocked the streetcar till it toppled.

"Steve, I thought your father was in the union," Tad said. "Why are you siding with the streetcar company?"

"I'm not siding with anybody," Steve said. "I'm just saying they didn't have to turn over two streetcars."

"They had to do something to get the attention of Thomas Lowry. My father says that Lowry won't even talk to the union leaders."

Steve made a face. "Do you really think that destroying a streetcar is going to make Lowry give the drivers back their wages? Lowry is not the kind of person to be frightened by something like that. In fact, it's likely to make him even angrier."

Rachel thought Steve had a good point. She watched as Jim Harrison could not hold his feelings in any longer. "If Lowry can do whatever he wants to do with the drivers' pay, then the drivers can do whatever they want with the streetcars."

Simon made a face. "Cutting the drivers' pay was a business decision. Lowry wasn't trying to hurt anybody."

"Maybe he didn't try to hurt anybody," Jim said, "but he did. All he cares about is making himself richer."

"It's his business. He has a right to make a profit."

Jim's face was flaming red now. "Does he have a right to take food away from my little sisters?"

"He didn't do that."

"Yes, he did!"

"No, he didn't."

Simon swung at Jim, who ducked just in time.

"Get 'em!" cried Tad. Rachel shook her head. That boy was always ready for a fight.

"Stop!" Hank shouted. "Please don't hurt each other. Please stop!"

But Jim's right fist connected with Simon's left eye.

Rachel gasped and jumped forward, but her brother was ahead of her. "Jim Harrison, stop this nonsense!" Sam grabbed Jim's arm and twisted it behind his back.

"He started it." Simon glared at Jim.

"No, I didn't."

"Yes, you did."

The bell rang just then. All across the school yard, students started shuffling their way into the building. Rachel joined them.

"We're not finished," she heard Simon mutter at Jim. Rachel looked over her shoulder and saw that Simon's eye was swelling up and had turned an angry red.

Jim scoffed. "Just remember who punched you."

A shadow fell across the ground in front of Rachel. She looked up to see Mr. Martin, the principal, looming over the students.

"I understand some of you boys were just involved in a dispute," he said in his deep, grave voice.

Rachel looked back at the boys. Jim and Simon stared straight ahead. Neither of them said anything.

"It is my understanding that this dispute centered on the riot last Sunday. Is that correct?"

Again, no one spoke. Mr. Martin frowned.

"Mr. Borland," the principal said. "And Miss Borland. I believe you both were present during the riot. Is that correct?"

Rachel swallowed hard. "Yes, sir," she heard Sam say, and she nodded silently.

Mr. Martin looked at Sam. "Were you participating, young man?"

"No, sir! We were on our way to Easter dinner, and we got trapped."

"So I understand. Perhaps you would like to comment for the other students on what you saw."

The mass of students had fallen silent. Rachel felt as though everyone was staring at her and her brother. She saw Sam gulp. "People were angry," he said softly.

"Please speak up, Mr. Borland," the principal said. "I want everyone here to be able to hear what you have to say."

Sam squared his shoulders. "People were angry," he repeated, almost shouting now. "They were saying mean things about each other—about their own neighbors. A few weeks ago it didn't matter that one friend was a manager at the mill and another friend drove a streetcar. But now, people are choosing their friends based on how they earn a living."

"And do you find this reasonable?" Mr. Martin asked.

Sam shook his head. "No, sir. It's not fair." Rachel saw him look at Simon and Jim. "A friend is a friend, no matter what."

Jim spoke up now. "But what if the friend you trusted does something to hurt you? Is he still a friend?"

Rachel watched as Sam thought for a moment. "I think that it is not always easy to understand why a person does something. And until we understand, we shouldn't get all riled up."

"Thank you, Mr. Borland," the principal said. "That is a very reasonable opinion. I would like everyone to spend some time today thinking about what Mr. Borland just said. And now, would you all please proceed immediately to your classrooms?"

Sam looked relieved to have attention shift away from him. Rachel caught his eye and smiled. "Good job," she mouthed, so only he would know what she was saying.

As the students jostled their way into the school building, Rachel noticed that Simon and Jim still did not look at each other. Had they listened to anything Sam said?

CHAPTER 15

A Birthday Blessing and a Tense Practice

Rachel woke up all at once on the first day of May, excited because of her birthday and yet a little worried because of her party. She had asked Annalina, Colleen, and Janie separately, and all had agreed to come. Colleen, Janie, and Rachel had spent their birthdays together in the past. Of course the cloud of the strike hadn't hung over them before.

"Happy birthday, Rachel!" Carrie screamed as Rachel came into the kitchen for breakfast. Carrie ran over and gave her now-eleven-year-old sister a big hug.

"Happy birthday, Rachel," Sam echoed, in a quieter, more dignified manner.

"Yes, honey, happy birthday," Rachel's parents greeted her in unison.

As Rachel sat down to her breakfast, she found two gifts at her place. "May I open them now, please?"

Her mother shrugged, "Well, I suppose so. But you must eat breakfast before you leave for school."

Rachel carefully pulled the paper from the first gift. "That's from Sam and me," piped up Carrie. She seemed more excited than Rachel. Inside the package was the most beautiful book Rachel had ever seen.

"It's a journal. The pages are all blank so you can write down all of your thoughts," Sam explained. "There's something else in there, too."

Rachel lifted up the journal and found a lovely pen. "Oh, Carrie and Sam. It's beautiful. I will think of both of you every time I write in the book."

Next she opened the gift from her mama and papa. It was a small package, but the paper and ribbon were so fancy.

"Oooh, it's so beautiful." Inside the package was a gold necklace with a small locket. Inside the locket was an even smaller lock of very fair-colored hair.

"That's your hair, Rachel. From when you were first born," Papa said.

"I've been saving it to give to you," her mama added. "To remind you how small you once were and how far you've come."

Rachel thought she was going to cry. "I love them all—I love you all. Thank you so much." She got up and walked around the table, hugging each member of her family.

Bringing everyone back to the present, Mama reminded everyone, "It's getting late. Now everyone eat your breakfast."

After what seemed to Rachel like forever, school finally ended for the day. Annalina came home with her, and Colleen and Janie arrived not long after. As Rachel had requested, her mother had made a small cake just for the girls.

All of the girls seemed a bit nervous, and Rachel thought that Annalina looked as though she felt out of place. "Let's eat cake first!" Rachel suggested. The others agreed, and they went into the kitchen. Mama had set the table with the nice plates, and she watched as Rachel cut the cake. After the girls got their cake, Mama left them alone for their own party.

"Annalina, this is 'cake.' Say it: 'cake.'"

"Cake!" Annalina said, smiling. Right the first time!

"That's right, Annalina. Colleen, Janie, she said 'cake.'" Rachel could not hide her enthusiasim.

Colleen and Janie looked at each other. Then they started giggling.

"Stop it!" Rachel said sharply to the two of them. "Annalina works hard to learn English. You shouldn't make fun of her." What Rachel had hoped would be the start of a renewed friendship was not off to a good start.

Colleen and Janie laughed harder. This time, Annalina joined them.

"What's going on?" Rachel could not believe what she was seeing—and hearing.

"It all right, Rachel," Annalina reassured her. "Colleen and Janie help me learn to say 'cake' to surprise you. We friend, too."

Colleen and Janie nodded. "Rachel, Janie and I decided that our friendship was too important to lose over something we could not control."

"Colleen and I agreed to disagree about the unions. After all, it's our parents' jobs, not ours. And we decided," Janie continued, putting her arm around Annalina, "that we should give Annalina a chance. After all, if you like her, there has to be a reason. Now, let's open your presents!"

For the second time that day, a gift had made Rachel feel like crying. She knew that what was in those packages could not be better than what Colleen, Janie, and Annalina had just given her.

That Saturday, Rachel followed Sam and her older cousin on their way to baseball practice.

"This is a terrific idea, Sam." Seth Stockard strode down the street next to his young cousin with a bat propped over his shoulder. At eighteen and a half, Seth was tall, with lanky legs and a long stride. His dark hair often looked like it needed to be combed.

"I promised the team you would say yes," Sam said, "so I'm sure glad you did."

"How could I say no to coaching a baseball team?"

"I thought you might be too busy. You have a job, and I know that you're really a scientist."

"I'm glad you recognize that, Sam, because I think it's time I started teaching you about science as well as baseball."

"Do you mean that?" Rachel saw the excitement on Sam's face, and she felt a twinge of jealousy. Sometimes it seemed like boys got to have all the fun. Then she remembered all the fun she and her friends had had at her birthday party, and she changed her mind. She knew her brother had had a tough time with his friends lately. He deserved to have some fun, too. "Can we work in your lab together?" Sam was asking Seth.

"Absolutely. But there's always time for baseball. You have a sharp team. I've seen you play. So I know this will be fun."

Sam sighed. "The last game was a disaster. I'm glad you weren't there. It was so embarrassing."

Seth chuckled. "I heard about it. It seems you lost your hurler. Has he come back to the team?"

"He was at practice on Tuesday, but I don't know if he'll come back today." Sam winced at the memory of Jim's fist hitting Simon's eye.

They turned a corner to head in the direction of the field.

"I know you can help us," Sam said. "But I have to warn you. Not everyone may want your help."

"Every coach has to win over some players—even on professional teams." Seth moved the bat to the other shoulder. "A good coach has to prove himself. I know I have to show that I understand baseball from the inside out."

If only it were that simple, Rachel thought. *If only the boys on the team would think about baseball and not unions and strikes.*

"You seem a little nervous," Rachel said, almost running to keep up with them.

Sam shrugged. "Getting a coach was my idea. Asking Seth was my idea. If—"

"If this doesn't work out, you'll look bad to the boys on your team." Seth finished Sam's thought. "Don't worry, Sam. I can make this work."

"How?"

"I'll just approach it scientifically. I'll make a hypothesis about what I think will happen, then I'll try some ideas to see if the hypothesis is true."

Rachel and Sam laughed.

By the time they arrived at the practice field, most of the boys were there already. Sam got their attention and signaled that they should gather around home plate. Rachel took her usual place on the bench.

"This is Seth Stockard, our new coach," Sam said proudly.

"Hello, boys."

"This is Jim. He plays first base." Sam pointed his finger at each boy in turn. "And this is Steve and Joe and Elwood and Larry, Tad, and Hank." Sam scanned the field. "I don't see Simon. He's the hurler."

"He's probably not coming," Joe said.

"He's just late," said Hank.

"No, he's not coming," Joe insisted.

Seth jumped in. "Let's give him a few minutes more. In the meantime, why don't we get started?"

"Just a minute." Steve was leaning on a bat with a suspicious expression on his face. "I have a few questions to ask the new coach."

"Sure," Seth said. "Ask anything you'd like."

"Have you ever coached a baseball team before?"

"No, but I've played baseball all my life. I taught Sam everything he knows."

That seemed to impress Steve. Rachel knew Sam was a good player.

"What position did you play?" Steve continued asking.

"Most of the time I played in the outfield. I have a pretty good arm for throwing the ball back into the infield."

"Can you hit?"

"Better than average," Seth said confidently. "I can get a hit when I really need one."

"How many professional games have you seen?"

"Oh, dozens, maybe hundreds," Seth answered. "I go whenever I can with my uncle Stanley."

"He's a railroad man, isn't he?" Joe asked.

"Yes, he is."

"Is he in the union?"

Rachel's stomach tightened. But she could see Seth was not flustered. "Hey, are we here to talk politics or to play ball?"

"Play ball!" exclaimed Tad.

"Then let's get to it." Seth clapped his hands several times. "You're going to have to show me what you can do today. Then we can work out some plays."

"What do you want us to do?" Sam asked.

"Set up a batting practice rotation," Seth answered. "I want to see your swings."

Sam nodded.

"Jim, go on over to first base," Seth said. "I'll pitch. The rest of you can get in the hitting rotation."

The boys set up their formation. Elwood batted first. Seth threw him an easy pitch, but it was a little high. Elwood let it pass.

"Good eye, good eye," Seth said.

He threw the next ball. This one was right down the center of the strike zone. Elwood swung. The ball bounced through the infield, an easy ground ball.

Seth stood behind Elwood. "Let's work on that swing for a minute," Seth said. They grasped the bat together. "You have a lot of power, Elwood. But your swing is not quite even. You're hitting the top of the ball. That's what makes it become a grounder."

Seth moved the bat to show what he meant.

"Keep your swing even, and you'll get the ball into the air." They swung together again. "It'll take a lot of practice, but you'll get it."

Rachel relaxed on her bench. The team seemed to be interested in what Seth had to say. But Simon was still missing. *Joe is probably right,* Rachel thought. Why would Simon come to play baseball after Jim had given him a black eye?

When she turned back to the boys, she saw that it was Tad's turn to bat. He grasped the bat at the very bottom and stood poised with his arms over the plate. Seth threw the pitch. Tad swung and hit the ball on the center of the bat. It was a line drive that lost its energy and plopped to the ground at second base.

"Good swing," Seth said. "Nice and even. But try stepping back from the plate a little bit. Then you can hit the ball with the end of the bat. It will have a lot more power and go farther."

Seth showed Tad where to stand, then pitched again. This time, Tad swung and belted the ball into right field. The team whooped its encouragement, and Rachel cheered, too.

In right field, Sam scooped up the ball and threw it back to Seth on the pitcher's mound. Tad had run safely to second base—something that almost never happened to Tad.

Rachel spotted Simon leaning against the fence. She waved and caught Sam's eye, then pointed toward Simon. Sam started to wave to Simon and seemed about to call him over. Then he apparently changed his mind. Rachel nodded to herself. If Simon wanted to play baseball, all he had to do was join the team.

Jim picked up a bat. Rachel knew that Jim had a straight, even swing. She wondered what Seth's comment would be.

Jim hit the first pitch. He threw the bat down awkwardly and started to run. The ball went to second base, where Hank snatched it up and threw it to first base. In a real game, Jim would have been out.

"Nice try, Jim," Seth said. "You have a nice swing. Let me just suggest one thing." He picked up a bat to demonstrate. "As you swing, start taking a step with your left foot. After you connect with the ball, let the bat swing around in your left hand and let it go. Don't worry about it. If you lift your foot on the swing, you'll be one step on your way to first base. You might have been able to beat out that throw."

Jim nodded. "I'll try that next time."

The batting practice continued. Steve and Joe and Hank took their turns. Seth diagnosed the swings of each player.

Rachel was keeping an eye on Simon. The hurler's hands had come out of the pockets of his trousers, and he had moved along the fence closer to the infield—closer to Seth. Rachel saw Simon listening carefully to everything Seth said.

"Now I want to see how well you can field," Seth called out to the team members. "I'll hit some fly balls. You try to catch them and throw them back in."

The team spread out around the field. Simon left the fence and joined the practice. He stood deep in left field only a few feet away from the fence. But he had definitely joined the practice.

Seth tossed a ball in the air and swung. The ball sailed into left field. Jim scrambled to get under the ball and held his hands high. Judging the arc of the ball carefully, he took a few steps back. The ball

plopped into his hands. Grinning, he heaved it back to the infield for
Seth to hit again.

"That was pretty good," Steve called out. "For someone who usually plays first base, you do pretty well in the outfield."

"Thanks!" Jim called back.

Rachel smiled to herself. If dolls and a birthday party could build
a bridge between enemies, maybe baseball could do the same.

When practice was over, Rachel trailed behind the boys as they
walked off the playing field toward their homes. "Your cousin is really
good," she heard Jim say to Sam. "I never noticed how I wasn't taking a step with my swing. That's really going to help."

"I've learned a lot from Seth," Sam said.

"You're lucky to have a cousin to teach you," Jim said.

"Jim is right." Simon had drifted over. "You're lucky to have Seth
teaching you, and now we're all lucky to have him coaching our team."

Rachel held her breath, watching as Simon and Jim started to talk
to each other.

"How's your eye?" Jim muttered.

"Not too bad."

"We thought you weren't coming."

"I thought about not coming."

"But you're here."

"This is my team," Simon said. "Where else am I going to go
to play?"

Jim shrugged. "The Seventh Street team would be happy to
have you."

"Naw. They don't have a coach."

Jim nodded. "You're right. We're the best. We have a coach."

"Even if he's a union man?" Simon asked.

"He's a ballplayer, through and through. That's what matters."

"Heads up!" Seth shouted. He tossed the ball toward the group. Rachel raised her eyes to the sky and tried to follow the path of the ball. She wanted to catch that ball, just to show the boys, but she knew she shouldn't spoil the moment by interfering.

Simon and Jim were also following the ball's arc, their heads tipped back. Neither of them were watching what the other was doing. Both of them jumped to catch the ball. Instead, they smacked into each other and tumbled into a heap. The ball dropped to the ground and dribbled past them.

The two boys broke into laughter. Untangling themselves, they lay on the ground, rubbing their heads where they had rammed into each other.

"I think you tripped me." Jim said, laughing.

"I'll probably have two black eyes now," Simon responded.

Rachel and Sam exchanged looks over the two boys' heads. Brother and sister smiled. Things were finally getting back to normal.

CHAPTER 16

A Disappointing Party

The doors opened and the children poured out of the school building into the bright sunshine of a May afternoon. Sam and Rachel met each other in their usual spot and looked around for Carrie. Rachel had promised Mama she would walk Carrie home.

"Rachel, look!" Carrie cried as she ran up to join them. "A streetcar!"

Rachel turned to look, and indeed a streetcar was rumbling past. At least ten passengers were riding inside. Now it was Rachel's turn to get excited.

"Sam, it's Janie's father. Mr. Lawrence is driving the streetcar!"

Sam looked carefully. "You're right. The strike must be over."

Mariah Webster was nearby. "The strike definitely is over," she informed them. "The drivers did not get their two cents an hour back. They have to work on Mr. Lowry's terms or not at all." Mariah tossed her hair over her shoulder haughtily.

"You don't have to be so excited," Sam said. "A lot of families got hurt during the strike."

"They caused all that trouble for nothing," Mariah retorted.

"The important thing is that it's over," Rachel said. "Everyone can go back to work, and things can go back to normal."

"I want to find Jim and talk to him," Sam said.

"You go ahead," Rachel said. "I'm going home. I have to finish getting ready for Annalina's party."

"Can I come to the party?" Carrie pleaded.

"I'm giving a birthday party for Annalina," Rachel said. "It's not for little kids."

"I'm not little, I'm eight."

"You'll have to be on your best behavior."

"I can behave, I promise."

"All right, then, but we have to hurry. I don't want Annalina to get there before we do." She turned and waved at Mariah. "See you at the party, Mariah."

Mariah did not answer.

Rachel and Carrie scurried toward home. They hadn't gotten far before they met Janie.

Janie was talking with some of the other girls in her class. Even Colleen was there.

"I saw your father driving," Rachel said. "I know he would never go against the union, so I guess this means the strike is over."

"It's over all right," grumbled Janie. "And Thomas Lowry won."

"I heard that the drivers didn't get the wage cut back."

"That's right. They got nothing. Thomas Lowry got it all, so he can stuff his fat, filthy pockets." Janie did not seem at all relieved that the strike was over.

"At least your father is working again," Rachel said.

"And the streetcars are running!" Katherine Jones was excited. "I was getting really tired of walking everywhere. I'm going to go downtown right now. I'm going to ride a streetcar all the way to Bridge Square and back."

"If you do," Janie said, "you're just putting more money in Thomas Lowry's pockets."

Rachel looked at Colleen, who had not said a word. *She could be gloating,* Rachel thought. *She could be boasting about the victory of Thomas Lowry.* But Colleen said nothing.

"A birthday pie?" Carrie asked, giggling. "I think that's silly!"

"It's what Annalina wanted," Rachel said. "Since she didn't get to eat pie when she came for supper, I promised to make her one for her birthday."

"Are you going to put candles in it?"

"Of course."

Carrie giggled again.

Rachel ignored Carrie and continued her preparations for the party. She had made the pie early in the morning before school, but she had not baked it yet. She wanted it to be fresh and hot from the oven for the party. Now it was time. She opened the oven and put the pie inside.

Then she turned her attention to the dining room. Mama had agreed to let Rachel have the party in the dining room. Annalina had never had a real birthday party before. Rachel wanted this party to be one Annalina would remember for a long time.

After the girls at school discovered Annalina's talent with the painted dolls, they seemed to welcome her a little more warmly. Rachel did not hear so many of them snickering behind Annalina's back. Katherine, especially, was intrigued by the dolls and wanted to learn to paint them herself. So Rachel had invited Mariah and Katherine and Phoebe and Beth to the party. Rachel had also invited Colleen and Janie, but they couldn't come. It was Colleen's father's birthday, and she had to spend the evening with her family. Janie was helping her mother. Janie told Rachel that her mother was getting stronger but was still too weak to make dinner without her help.

Pink was Annalina's favorite color, so last night, Rachel had decorated the dining room with as much pink as she could find, from the tablecloth to paper streamers tied to the lights. A big sign propped up on the buffet read HAPPY BIRTHDAY, ANNALINA. Rachel's gift for Annalina was wrapped in pink tissue paper and placed in the center of the table.

A knock sounded at the front door. Carrie jumped up. "I'll get it."

"I early?" Annalina asked. Her cheeks were pink.

"Did you run all the way?" Carrie asked.

Annalina nodded.

"You're right on time," Rachel answered. "The others will be here soon. Now close your eyes."

Annalina looked puzzled. Rachel put her hands over Annalina's eyes, making her friend giggle. She led Annalina into the dining room. There, she removed her hands. The Swedish girl gasped. "Pretty! For me?"

"Yes, it's for you," Rachel said smiling. "Happy birthday, Annalina."

Annalina spun around and hugged Rachel. "Dank you, dank you, Rachel."

Carrie nudged her way in between them. "Where are the other girls?" she asked.

"They're coming," Rachel said confidently. "We just got out of school. They probably had to go home and get their gifts for Annalina."

"Will you braid my hair while you wait?" Carrie asked Annalina.

Rachel looked to be sure Annalina had understood. Annalina was already separating Carrie's hair into the strands that would become twin braids.

The clock in the hall ticked loudly. Rachel tried not to look at it too often. She was no longer sure the other girls were coming. Rachel watched as Annalina nimbly braided Carrie's hair. Carrie was sitting perfectly still. It would not be long at all before the job was done, but for once, Rachel wished that Carrie would wiggle a little bit. But Carrie had promised to be on her best behavior, and she was.

The clock ticked.

Finally someone knocked on the door. Rachel leaped out of her chair and ran to open the door.

"Katherine! Hello!"

"Hello, Rachel." Katherine stood on the front porch awkwardly holding a small package. She wore a emerald green satin dress that highlighted her eyes beautifully. Rachel had never seen her look so lovely, but she had not expected Katherine to change from her cotton school frock into such a fancy dress.

"Come in." Rachel opened the door wide. She glanced over her shoulder at the dining room, grinning. "Where are the others?"

Katherine shuffled into the house. "I'm not sure," she muttered.

Rachel was puzzled. "Didn't you talk to Mariah today—or Phoebe or Beth? They were all in school today."

Katherine licked her lips nervously. "I don't think they're coming," she said quietly.

Rachel closed the door and leaned against it. "What do you mean?"

"I asked them all if they were coming," Katherine said, "because I can't stay. I wanted someone to bring my gift."

"You can't stay?" Rachel asked.

"My mother says I have to go have dinner at my grandmother's house. My aunt just got engaged, and they're having a party for her tonight. Mama's waiting out in the carriage."

"So that's why you're in your best dress."

"I'm sorry, Rachel."

"It's all right, Katherine. You have to do what your mother wants you to do."

"I'm sorry about the others, too."

"That's not your fault," Rachel said.

"Here, please give this to Annalina." Katherine put the small package in Rachel's hands.

"Don't you want to say happy birthday to Annalina yourself?"

"My mother is waiting. We have to go look for my brother, Steve."

"But, Katherine—"

"I'm sorry. I have to go."

Then she was gone. Rachel turned back to the dining room. Determined not to let Annalina see the disappointment she felt, she marched into the room.

"Look what Katherine brought for you," she said brightly.

"Where is Katherine?" Carrie asked.

"She couldn't stay," Rachel explained. "She had to go to her aunt's engagement party."

"Katherine go?" Annalina looked puzzled.

Rachel nodded. "She wanted to stay, but she couldn't."

Annalina did not respond. Her lower lip quivered.

"I think it's time we get this party started," Rachel said.

"But no one's here," Carrie commented.

Rachel shot her sister a pointed look. "We're here," she said emphatically. "We don't need a whole roomful of people in order to have a party."

"They're not coming, are they?" Carrie said. "They didn't want to come to Annalina's party."

Rachel wanted to give her sister a good shake and send her out of the room. "That just means more pie for us," Rachel said.

But Annalina was not fooled. She had understood enough of what Carrie said to know that no one was coming to her birthday party. She sank into a chair. "Girls not come," she said sadly.

Rachel said quietly, "No, the other girls are not coming."

Annalina set Katherine's gift on the table next to Rachel's. "They not like me."

"They don't know you," Rachel insisted. "If they would get to know you, they would like you as much as I do."

Annalina stared at the floor.

"Let's open the gifts," Carrie suggested.

"That's a wonderful idea." Rachel sat down next to Annalina and once again put the package from Katherine in her hands.

Slowly, Annalina unwrapped the box and opened it. Inside lay a neat row of six bright paint colors and two new brushes. Annalina's face brightened. "New paint! I need!"

"That was a thoughtful gift," Rachel said.

"Open Rachel's present," Carrie urged. From the other side of the table, she nudged the package toward Annalina.

Annalina gently removed three layers of pink tissue paper and opened her mouth in delight. "Pretty!" She held up one of twelve colorful ribbons, two each of six different colors.

"I got them from Mr. Johanssen's shop," Rachel explained. "I'll have to take you there. But maybe you already know him. He's Swedish, too, after all. He has lovely things in his shop. He might even like to sell your dolls. Your father could carve them, you could paint them, and Mr. Johanssen can sell them." She clapped her hands in delight at her own idea. "I'll talk to him right away."

Annalina laughed. She had not understood much of Rachel's speech. "Rachel talk much," she said.

"How is the party going?" Mama had just appeared in the doorway.

Annalina smiled at Mama. "Presents nice."

"I'm glad you like them."

"Is it time for pie?" Carrie asked eagerly.

Rachel glanced at the clock. "It should be just about done."

Mama sniffed the air. "It doesn't smell like you're baking a pie."

Rachel's stomach sank. Mama was right. By now the house ought to be filled with the aroma of sweetened fruit. She jumped out of her chair and dashed into the kitchen.

Pulling the oven door open, she looked at her pie. It was formed perfectly. But it was still pasty white and raw. She groaned.

"I forgot to ask you to light the oven," she said to Mama. "It should have been baking all this time."

"I'll light the oven now," Mama offered.

"It's too late," Rachel said. "Annalina has to go home soon."

Carrie and Annalina came into the kitchen.

"What's wrong with the pie this time?" Carrie asked.

Rachel's face crumpled.

"The pie is perfect," Mama said, "it's just not baked."

"No pie?" Annalina asked, confused.

Rachel shook her head. "No pie." She opened the oven door and showed Annalina. Instantly, Annalina understood. She started giggling.

"Why are you laughing?" Rachel said. "I've ruined your party. We don't have a cake or a pie or anything."

Annalina giggled some more. Carrie started laughing, too. And then Mama started.

"What's so funny?" Rachel demanded.

"If this were a baseball game," Carrie said, "you'd be out on three strikes. This is the third pie you've made that no one got to eat."

Now Rachel started laughing. "Three strikes or not, I'm not quitting," she said. "Someday I will make a pie, and we will all eat it!"

CHAPTER 17

Friends at Last

Rachel arrived at the baseball field early. She was one of the first spectators to claim a seat, so she made herself comfortable on the wooden bench along the first-base line. She arranged her blue calico dress so that it fell evenly around her knees and ankles and tucked in her shawl so it would not flap in the breeze. Her hair, braided carefully that morning, featured matching white ribbon bows.

Rachel leaned forward to study the activities of the players. The Spitfires were warming up on the field, while the Oak Lake Boaters were having batting practice.

Gradually more people came to watch the game. A few parents settled themselves on benches or quilts in the grass. Many of the spectators were brothers and sisters of the players.

Out of the corner of her eye, Rachel saw Mariah Webster strolling across the field beside Beth. Rachel turned her head to watch them more closely. Usually Mariah and Beth and Phoebe came to baseball games with Katherine Jones. Katherine came to watch her brother Steve, but Katherine was not with Mariah today.

Mariah tossed her hair haughtily as she approached Rachel. The bench was empty except for Rachel, who sat perched at one end, but Mariah and Beth did not pause.

"Hello, Mariah. Hello, Beth," Rachel said in her sweetest voice. "It's a fine day for a game, don't you think?"

Mariah rolled her eyes. "I suppose." She kept walking right past

Rachel. Without speaking to Rachel, Beth followed Mariah to a patch of grass behind first base. There they put their heads together and giggled.

Rachel was determined not to be annoyed. She turned her attention back to the field.

Sam fielded a ball Seth had tossed toward him. In one smooth motion, Sam scooped it out of the dirt, twisted, and snapped the ball to Jim, waiting on first base. Jim grinned and delivered the ball to Simon on the pitcher's mound.

Abe signaled that the team should gather together. With his arms around the shoulders of Sam and Larry, Seth smiled proudly at all the Spitfires.

"You boys have been working very hard," he said. "In a few minutes, all your hard work is going to pay off."

"That's right," Elwood said. "The Oak Lake Boaters will not even know what hit them."

"Simon and Jim," Seth said, "do you remember the play we went over?"

Simon nodded enthusiastically. "If I see a runner taking a lead off of first base, I fire at Jim."

"And I keep my foot on the base so I'm always ready," Jim added. "We won't let any base runners get past us."

"Joe and Sam, are you ready for the double-play balls?" Seth asked.

"Better than ever," Sam answered.

"And you've all been working on your swings. Keep your eye on the ball and stay steady."

Hank and Elwood practiced swinging imaginary bats.

"Hey," Hank said, "where's Steve? We need him to help cover the outfield."

The whole team turned to scan the playing field.

"There he is," Larry called out, pointing at left field.

Rachel saw Steve trotting across the field with Katherine dragging behind him.

"Sorry I'm late!" Steve called out.

"We're just glad you're here," Jim said. "We need everybody today."

"Let's play ball!" Seth said, clapping his hands. The team scattered to take their positions.

Katherine hurried to get out of the way of the players. "Hi, Katherine!" Rachel called. "Come sit with me."

Mariah and Beth burst into laughter. "Of course she's not going to sit with you," Mariah said. "What makes you think such a thing? Come on, Katherine, there's plenty of room for you over here."

Rachel paid no attention to Mariah. She kept her eyes fixed on Katherine, whose steps were slowing down.

"I'd like to hear about your aunt's engagement party," Rachel said. "I'm sure everyone loved the dress you wore."

Katherine hesitated for just a moment. Then she turned her steps toward Rachel. She came and sat on the bench. Rachel could hear Mariah gasp in the background.

"Don't pay any attention to her," Rachel advised.

"I won't," Katherine said. "I should have stopped following Mariah Webster around a long time ago."

"How was the engagement party?"

"It was nice. There were lots of sweet cakes and punch. But I kept wishing I was at Annalina's birthday party."

"Really and truly?"

"Really and truly. You're right about Annalina. She's nice. I like her. I'm sorry for making fun of her."

"She'll be glad to hear that," Rachel said. "She's supposed to meet me here later."

Katherine turned her eyes to the field. "It looks like the game is about to start."

Rachel turned toward the field as well. She saw that Simon was studying the batter. With his left arm, he leaned on his knee. His right arm, with the ball in his hand, was tucked behind his back. Finally, he stood up straight, wound up, and threw the first pitch of the game.

It was a strike, straight and true. The batter swung and missed. The ball smacked into the hands of Tad Leland, the catcher. With a whoop, Tad threw the ball back to Simon.

From the sideline, Seth caught Simon's eye. Rachel held her breath as Simon nodded, indicating he had understood Seth's secret message. Simon got ready for the next pitch. The batter swung again, scraping the top of the ball with his bat and sending it dribbling into the infield. Sam easily stopped the rolling ball and threw it to Jim before the batter could get to first base.

Seth paced along the sideline, clapping his hands. "That's the way to do it, boys!"

"It looks like they're off to a good start," Katherine commented. "Steve was a little worried on the way over here."

"That's because they lost so badly the last time," Rachel said. "Simon wasn't here to hurl. But with Simon pitching and Jim Harrison playing first base, the other team doesn't have a chance."

Katherine smiled. "I hope you're right. But it's only the first inning."

"Go Spitfires!" Rachel shouted.

"Beat the Boaters!" screamed a voice just behind her. Rachel turned to see Mariah Webster standing behind the bench. Rachel stared up at Mariah with questions in her eyes.

"The ground is cold," Mariah said. "You said there was plenty of room on the bench."

"There still is."

Katherine scooted closer to Rachel. Mariah and Beth sat down.

"If you're going to sit here," Katherine said, "you have to promise not to be mean."

Mariah tilted her head, puzzled.

"I don't want you saying anything nasty about Annalina or Rachel or anybody."

Mariah didn't seem to know what to say. "I promise," she finally said.

"Here comes Annalina!" Rachel cried. "We have room on the bench for one more, don't we?"

"Of course!" Katherine responded.

But Annalina wasn't alone. Colleen and Janie were with her.

Annalina's steps slowed as she approached the first-base line. Now she stopped. She caught Rachel's eyes with her own worried ones.

Rachel waved to Annalina. "It's all right, Annalina. Come and sit with us."

Annalina did not move.

"What's the matter with her?" Mariah asked.

Katherine scowled. "Would you want to come and sit with people who have been as mean to you as we've been to her?"

Mariah hung her head. "No, I guess not."

Biting her lower lip, Annalina looked from Rachel to Katherine to Mariah. She still did not move her feet.

Rachel waved her arm in a big circle. "Come on, Annalina, Colleen, Janie. Come and sit."

Colleen and Janie took seats on the bench. Still Annalina did not move.

Katherine stood up. "I'm going to get her."

Rachel grinned and watched. Katherine marched over to Annalina and took the Swedish girl by the hand. She pulled so hard that Annalina had no choice but to follow. Katherine led Annalina to the bench and pointed to the open spot between Mariah and Beth.

Gingerly, Annalina sat down. She looked around nervously.

"It's all right," Katherine said. "We want to be your friends."

"Friends?"

"Yes, friends, just like Rachel is your friend."

"Rachel is friend."

"Yes, Rachel is your friend. And so am I."

Annalina smiled nervously. Katherine glared at Mariah and Beth.

Awkwardly, Mariah leaned over and put a hand on Annalina's shoulder. "Sit with us whenever you want to. We're glad to have you."

Confused, Annalina turned to Rachel for reassurance.

Rachel was smiling so big she could hardly talk. "It's all right, Annalina. It's not a trick. We all want you to sit with us, to be our friend." It felt right. Her old friends had joined with her new friend. Now they were all just friends, the way it should be.

The crack of a bat made them turn their heads back to the game. The ball sailed to center field. Steve Jones was under it and snatched it out of the air.

CHAPTER 18

Peace in the Family

Carrie twirled to make her pink dress spin. "Do you like my pretty dress, Papa?" she asked.

"You look spectacular." Papa sat on the sofa in the living room, Rachel next to him, and Sam in the chair across from him.

"I didn't get to wear my new Easter dress to Aunt Linda's for Easter dinner, so I decided to wear it today."

"You made a good choice," Papa said.

Rachel watched Carrie's spinning dress and thought of her own new sapphire cloak. It had not survived the Easter Sunday riot as well as Carrie's dress had. She only got to wear the new cloak one day. Then it was so tattered that it went straight to the rag pile. Still, Rachel was happy that Carrie was enjoying her new dress.

"Are Uncle Ernest and Uncle Stanley going to argue?" Carrie asked somberly. "Are they going to shout and be mad like they were when they were here?"

Papa pulled Carrie onto his knee. "I can't promise you what anyone will do. But I do think Stanley and Ernest are trying to get along better these days."

"The strike is over, so they don't have to fight about that," Carrie said. Papa nodded.

"Freddy says that his papa quarrels with Uncle Ernest all the time."

"I don't think they quarrel all the time," Papa said slowly. "But they do have different opinions about many things."

"They can get along if they want to," Sam said. "Look at Jim and Simon. A couple weeks ago they were so angry they were hitting each other. But now they get along again."

"And Mariah and Annalina are starting to be friends," Rachel added. "Mariah thinks Annalina is really smart. Once she stopped making fun of her, she found out how much she likes Annalina."

"And Ernest and Stanley like each other, too," Papa said. "I'm sure of that. They've known each other for a long time."

"I'm glad we're going to have a family dinner to make up for Easter," Carrie said.

Mama entered the room. "Rachel, your pie is ready to come out of the oven. As soon as you wrap it up, we can be on our way to the Stockards'."

Sam snickered. "Are we going to get to eat this pie, Rachel?"

"This pie is perfect," Rachel declared. "I was very careful with the recipe."

A few minutes later, the Borland family was walking down the street, laden with their part of the family dinner. Rachel, of course, carried her cherry pie carefully and proudly. It was wrapped in two towels to keep it extra safe. Carrie swung a basket of biscuits, Sam lugged a sack of potatoes, Papa had the corn pudding, and Mama had the apple pie.

"Are we going to ride a streetcar?" Carrie asked.

"Here comes one now," Sam said.

"It's Mr. Lawrence's car." Rachel waved her arm to signal that the car should stop for them.

They clambered aboard and settled into seats right behind Mr. Lawrence.

"How are you all?" Turning to Sam, and nudging the horses forward, Mr. Lawrence said, "I hear you hit quite a long ball against the Oak Lake team."

Sam smiled proudly. "It was a triple. Two runs scored on my hit."

"How is Mrs. Lawrence?" Mama asked."

"Well, it seems as though she has turned the corner. She's doing much better, thank you." Glancing at Rachel, he added, "I suppose Janie will have more free time for recipe swapping."

Rachel smiled. "Well, the last time we tried it things didn't go so well. I'm willing to try again."

"Why are you carrying around half a market?" Mr. Lawrence asked, eyeing their food.

"We're going to have Easter dinner," Carrie explained.

Mr. Lawrence chuckled. "Well, that's a fine idea. There was quite a bit of excitement that day, wasn't there?"

"We're going to the Stockards'," Carrie said.

"Ah, yes, I hear their son Seth is coaching your team," Mr. Lawrence said to Sam. When he saw the puzzled expression on Sam's face, he laughed. "When you drive a streetcar you hear all kinds of things."

They got off the streetcar in front of the Stockards' house. Carrie scampered up the steps and knocked on the door ahead of the rest of them. When it opened, she hurtled through, calling for Freddy.

Aunt Linda stood in the open doorway with Aunt Agnes right behind her. They both laughed at Carrie. Mama shook her head.

"When she gets excited," Mama said, "there's just nothing I can do to control her."

"Is everyone here?" Rachel asked.

Aunt Linda nodded. "Molly and Miranda are upstairs. No doubt they're talking about their latest beaus. Seth and Gage are out back in Seth's old lab."

"What about Uncle Ernest—and Uncle Stanley?" Rachel was almost too nervous to ask.

"Hmm," Aunt Linda said, puzzled. "I'm not sure where they disappeared to."

"These potatoes are heavy," Sam complained.

Aunt Linda took them from him. "Let's put the food in the kitchen. Rachel, your pie smells delicious. I can't wait to taste it."

Rachel and Mama followed Aunt Linda into the kitchen, where Aunt Agnes was stirring her currant glaze in a pan on top of the stove. She smiled to welcome them.

"The ham smells wonderful!" Rachel said as she set her pie down on the table and began unwrapping it.

Aunt Agnes bent over and peeked at the ham in the oven. "It will be done in just a few minutes."

"I'll start peeling potatoes." Mama took the sack from Aunt Linda.

"Agnes," Aunt Linda said, "do you know what happened to Stanley?"

"He was headed for the study the last time I saw him," Aunt Agnes replied.

Aunt Linda raised her eyebrows. "Ernest's study?"

"Yes."

"Ernest was in there reading the last time I saw him."

Mama and Rachel exchanged a worried glance.

Aunt Linda read their minds. "Perhaps I'll just go check and see how things are in the study."

"I'll go with you," Rachel said.

As they approached the open study door, they heard rising voices.

"What on earth made you think to do such a thing?" Uncle Stanley exclaimed.

"I'm simply using the mind that God gave me," Uncle Ernest answered. "I suggest you do the same."

"Oh, no!" Rachel said. By now, Mama and Aunt Agnes had heard the voices and followed them into the hallway. Papa and Sam left the living room and joined the growing huddle in the hall.

"Should we go in?" Mama asked.

"They have to work things out themselves," Aunt Linda insisted.

"They may need a little help." Papa stepped through the doorway. Then, he tilted his head back and roared with laughter.

"Papa, what is it?" Rachel asked anxiously.

Papa gestured that they should all come in. The two men sat across the desk from each other. Between them was a chessboard. Most of the white pieces had been captured, and the king was checkmated. Uncle Ernest had the smirk of victory on his face.

"We haven't been playing more than ten minutes," Uncle Stanley complained, "and already he's thrashed me."

Rachel laughed in relief.

Uncle Stanley pointed a finger at his brother-in-law. "This is not the end of it, my friend. I learn from my mistakes. You will not win so easily the next time."

"We all learn from our mistakes," Uncle Ernest said quietly. "Let us pray that the city of Minneapolis—even the whole country—can learn from its mistakes."

Uncle Stanley nodded. "This nation has too much potential not to learn from its mistakes. If Jim Hill can build a railroad that reaches all the way to the West Coast, the rest of us can learn to solve our problems together."

Uncle Ernest chuckled. "May I remind you that Jim Hill has not reached the West Coast yet?"

Uncle Stanley grinned in response. "It won't be long, now."

Rachel caught Sam's eye and saw the smile on his face. The two men were bantering the way they always had. But the lightness in their tone and the twinkle in their eyes made everyone relax.

"I'd better get back to the potatoes," Mama said.

"Oh, the glaze is probably boiling by now," Aunt Agnes added.

"Rachel, I'm saving room for a piece of your pie," Uncle Stanley put in.

Rachel smiled. "I'm afraid it's only one pie. It's not enough for fourteen people." She turned and headed for the kitchen.

"Well, I'm having a piece," Sam declared. "After all, you've made four pies and we haven't gotten to eat any of them yet."

"This pie made it all the way over here, safe and sound." Rachel pushed open the kitchen door. "As soon as dinner's over—"

White-faced, Rachel gasped and spun around to Sam.

"What is it?" Sam pushed past his sister and burst into the kitchen.

Freddy and Carrie sat at the table with cherries smeared on their faces and soiled forks in their hands.

"We were hungry," Freddy explained.

Rachel was too shocked to speak. Her beautiful pie was half-eaten. The remaining half was so crumbled that no one would want to eat it.

Sam roared with laughter. "I guess I'll have to wait for pie number five!"

If you enjoyed

Rachel
and the Riot

be sure to read other

SISTERS IN TIME

books from BARBOUR PUBLISHING

- Perfect for Girls Ages Eight to Twelve

- History and Faith in Intriguing Stories

- Lead Character Overcomes Personal Challenge

- Covers Seventeenth to Twentieth Centuries

- Collectible Series of Titles

6" x 8 ¼" / Paperback / 144 pages / $3.97

AVAILABLE WHEREVER CHRISTIAN BOOKS ARE SOLD.